DISCARDED LAWYER (BUT NOT DEAD YET)

By Donald W. Desaulniers

DISCARDED LAWYER (BUT NOT DEAD YET)

PAPERBACK ISBN: 978-1-989683-18-7

TABLE OF CONTENTS

DISCARDED LAWYER (BUT NOT DEAD YET) 1
TABLE OF CONTENTS 2
CHAPTER 1 (Outvoted and Ousted) 6
CHAPTER 2 (Liquid Retirement Party) 12
CHAPTER 3 (Escaping New York) 16
CHAPTER 4 (On the Road) 21
CHAPTER 5 (House Purchase) 25

CHAPTER 6 (Surrounded by Color) 32
CHAPTER 7 (Quiet Christmas Break) 37
CHAPTER 8 (One Solitary Client) 40
CHAPTER 9 (Tough Breaks) 43
CHAPTER 10 (Making My First Enemy) 49
CHAPTER 11 (Insurance Sharks) 53
CHAPTER 12 (First Contact) 57
CHAPTER 13 (Hick Lawyer) 61
CHAPTER 14 (Negative Opinion) 68
CHAPTER 15 (Easy Money) 71
CHAPTER 16 (Motion Aftermath) 77
CHAPTER 17 (A Blunt Advocate) 80
CHAPTER 18 (A Dog's Breakfast) 85
CHAPTER 19 (Vivacious Company) 90
CHAPTER 20 (Angry Rich Guy) 95
CHAPTER 21 (Wrapping Up the File) 106
CHAPTER 22 (First Date) 111
CHAPTER 23 (Rapid Treachery) 117
CHAPTER 24 (Complaint Settled) 121
CHAPTER 25 (More Treachery) 126
CHAPTER 26 (Complaint Number Two) 130
CHAPTER 27 (Closing Up Shop) 135
CHAPTER 28 (Ultimate Treachery) 139
CHAPTER 29 (Investigation) 144
CHAPTER 30 (Sorting Out the Mess) 152
CHAPTER 31 (On the Road Again) 159
CHAPTER 32 (Getting my Bearings) 164
CHAPTER 33 (A New Friend) 168
CHAPTER 34 (Startling Developments) 171
CHAPTER 35 (Money Talks) 174
CHAPTER 36 (Long Trip) 179
CHAPTER 37 (Unwelcome) 182
CHAPTER 38 (Surprises) 185
CHAPTER 39 (Motive Established) 192
CHAPTER 40 (Courtroom Terror) 198
CHAPTER 41 (Las Vegas Bound) 204

ABOUT THE AUTHOR..207

CHAPTER 1 (Outvoted and Ousted)

My senior secretary poked her head in my office at quarter to five.

"Sir, there's an emergency meeting taking place at five o'clock in the main conference room and your presence is required."

"That's news to me, Diane. Do you know what it's about?"

"No sir, I don't."

I finished what I was doing on my computer and closed it down for the night.

Normally I worked until at least seven but this unexpected meeting would almost certainly waste the rest of my standard workday.

Please allow me to introduce myself.

My full name is Donald Carl Saunders but everyone calls me Carl. I'm sixty-six and the senior partner in a smallish law firm in Buffalo, New York. I've been divorced for twenty-five years but fortunately with no children.

At the moment I was renting a small furnished condominium apartment in a high-rise building just two blocks from the law office. My tenancy was still weekly even though I'd now lived in this one-bedroom unit for almost a year.

I sold my own townhouse condo in December of 2019 including my furniture because I felt that real estate prices had exploded into an unsustainable bubble which would eventually burst. I had also grown tired of commuting to work every day.

When the coronavirus pandemic hit America in March of 2020 I was certain that I'd made the correct decision about selling but so far I'd been proven wrong. Real estate prices had risen significantly over the past year.

It wasn't the first time I'd been completely wrong and certainly wouldn't be the last.

Today was Thursday, the 17th of December and the Covid-19 travel restrictions had persuaded me not to take a Christmas trip down to Las Vegas. This would be the first Christmas in many years that I'd remained in Buffalo.

As I walked down the hallways to the main conference room, I wondered if my partners were still in a snit about two recent issues which had become somewhat contentious.

My four fellow partners had wanted to move into more upscale office space. Our existing lease in this building had expired at the end of October. We were currently at an impasse in the firm's decision about our space and were now just month-to-month tenants.

My reasoning had been that committing ourselves either to new office space or a fixed term renewal of our lease on this space was foolhardy. The economic shutdowns were decimating all sorts of businesses and once the government assistance ended, I was certain that office rents would plummet as scads of commercial tenants vacated their office spaces and closed their operations.

The other issue dealt with a potential new client. Harold Axelrod, the partner next in line in seniority to me, had wined and dined the executives of an insurance company. Harold had convinced them to move their litigation over to our firm.

When he raised the matter at our last partners' meeting a week ago, I had objected quite strenuously. I'd researched the company on the internet and elsewhere and quickly discovered that they were obscenely aggressive in denying claims.

Our firm was doing just fine financially so I exercised my senior partner veto power over new clients and rejected the insurance sharks.

Harold was alone in the conference room when I walked in a few minutes before five o'clock. He already had an alcoholic drink in his hand, a habit of his I loathed. Drinking on the job even at lunchtime was a recipe for negligence. Few guys could maintain their mental sharpness after socking back a couple of drinks.

I greeted Harold in a friendly manner and asked what the meeting was about.

He evaded an answer and simply replied that the others should arrive momentarily.

We talked about the Buffalo Bills for a moment. They were fighting for a playoff spot, something which had eluded the team for a long time.

The other partners wandered in together. Clyde Jackson, Karen Josephson and Marie Clairmont were all in their forties. Harold was only fifty-one.

Within two minutes the hammer fell.

Harold convened the meeting and advised that there was only one matter to be dealt with this evening.

He thereupon handed me a document which I read with more than a bit of shock and horror.

My partners were exercising their rights under our partnership agreement to boot me out of the firm immediately.

I never saw this scenario unfolding.

The compensation clause was crystal clear in our agreement. I would receive a buy-out based on a percentage of my average billings over the previous four calendar years.

Karen was the first to speak.

"This is a letter confirming your billings during the years 2016 through 2019 inclusive along with a bank draft payable to you for the duly calculated buyout."

It was all business. The fact that we had practiced law together for many years wasn't even acknowledged.

Clyde threw in his two cents' worth.

"Since your own name isn't included in this firm's name, the only changes we need to make are to take your name off the firm's letterhead and have you sign off on your firm computer and smart phone."

"What about my ongoing files?"

Harold responded.

"We'll take over carriage of them immediately. The partnership agreement is clear on that issue. As soon as you release control of your computer and smart phone to the firm, you're effectively retired at least as far as practising law in Buffalo is concerned. As I'm sure you're aware, our agreement contains a non-competition clause."

My partners were correct. There was no point fighting them.

I smiled.

"I guess this means hello retirement. Let's sign these termination documents and then get the computer and smart phone matters dealt with right away at which point I'll walk off into the sunset."

We all signed the various legal documents. Harold couldn't suppress a self-satisfied smirk. He was now the top dog.

We went single-file like a funeral procession back to my office where I provided my personal passwords and waited while the firm changed the passwords and then confirmed that the new ones worked and my old ones did not.

I shook everyone's hand and wished them success. Marie handed me a cardboard box and I loaded my personal photos and knickknacks into it.

They confiscated my office keys and escorted me out the office door.

I took the elevator down to the lobby. There were no cabs around so I lugged the cardboard box home on foot.

It was just a few minutes before seven o'clock.

In less than two hours I had been outvoted and ousted.

CHAPTER 2 (Liquid Retirement Party)

As soon as I got inside my apartment, I went directly to the refrigerator and cracked open a beer.

Drinking was perfectly acceptable after work. In fact few attorneys could survive without their evening booze.

I'd been numb on my demeaning walk home but after a few swigs of beer, I began to focus.

It had been a treacherous move on the part of my partners. They had orchestrated the ouster completely behind my back. I suspected that they had been planning the move ever since our last partner meeting.

There was no point being bitter about it. The others were a fair bit younger than me and wanted to expand. I had been satisfied with the status quo.

I pulled the bank draft out of my wallet and examined it. Suddenly I was $478,000 wealthier in liquid assets. Surely that fact would reduce the humiliation factor of being booted out of my own law firm.

I wondered where the partners had come up with the money to buy me out. I hadn't socialized with any of them and really knew very little about their personal lives.

Tomorrow I'd deposit the bank draft and then decide whether to invest the money. I had been whittling down my stock portfolio in the past two months. For a while earlier in the year, the stock markets had tanked and on paper I had suffered a significant loss.

Thankfully the markets recovered and were now hovering in record territory. I planned on dumping the rest of my stocks in January.

With both real estate and stocks on the verge of a bursting bubble, I'd probably leave my money in cash despite the abysmal interest rates.

I was a prudent and conservative guy. Perhaps that was another reason why my partners decided to throw me under the bus. All four of them were risk takers.

By the time I was half way through my third can of beer, it struck me that Buffalo no longer held any appeal.

My best friend had died three years ago and my career had been my sole focus since then.

As I pondered my future, the idea floated up that now would be an ideal time to ditch Buffalo and start a new life elsewhere.

I had grown up in the small town of Wellsville in Upstate New York about seventy-five miles southeast of Buffalo.

My parents were now both deceased and I'd been their only child so I had no close relatives left in Wellsville or anywhere else.

The thought crossed my mind that perhaps I could set up my law practice in my home town. I pulled out my copy of the partnership agreement and noted with annoyance that the non-competition clause prevented me from practising law anywhere in New York State. It wasn't just restricted to the city of Buffalo.

That eliminated the possibility of setting up shop in Wellsville.

Realizing that my legal career was truly over was a very sobering and surprisingly depressing thought.

I didn't feel ready to retire yet.

The remainder of my retirement party consisted of tossing back three more cans of beer and looking through a box of old photographs from my university days and from my eleven year marriage to Beth.

It struck me that it couldn't have been easy for Beth to be married to me. Like most young attorneys, I was fixated on my career. Eventually we drifted apart and split up. There was no acrimony. I had chosen career over marriage. Beth remarried a couple of years later and moved to Florida. We never had contact after that.

Lawyers weren't good marriage material. They made lots of money which meant an upscale life but toiling away at a law office for roughly eighty hours each week left no time or energy for a spouse.

It was a shame that Beth and I hadn't realized that truth before we tied the knot.

Although I never cheated on Beth or abused her in any way, I'd been a lousy husband, blinded by some complex combination of ambition and greed.

By the time I poured myself into bed, I was severely morose.

Carl Saunders had first been a failure as a marriage partner and now had become the latest victim of a surprise hostile takeover.

CHAPTER 3 (Escaping New York)

A nasty hangover greeted me on Friday morning.

Unfortunately I woke by long-standing habit at six-thirty in the morning.

Normally I hit the office by seven-thirty.

Today I remained in bed feeling sorry for myself.

Any visions I had harbored of a festive retirement party at the end of my legal career attended by throngs of my fellow attorneys and office staff had been unceremoniously snatched away.

The only attendees had been bad memories, the most recent being the surreptitious escort out of the office like a vile leper by the very attorneys I had worked with and mentored for many years.

Finally I crawled out of bed at nine o'clock, showered, dressed and ate a simple breakfast of toast and cereal.

My rent was due every Saturday.

I dutifully wrote the check and would drop it in to the building superintendent on my way to my bank later this morning.

The box of mementos was still on the coffee table in the living-room along with an honor guard of empty beer cans.

As I began putting the photos back in the box, I spotted a street map of Wichita, Kansas.

For a moment I wondered what that was doing in with my college and marriage pictures.

I picked up the map and unfolded it to take a closer look. A business card fell out onto the carpet.

I picked up the card and was for a moment confused.

It was my own business card bearing just my name, a cell phone number and the statement "ATTORNEY-AT-LAW LICENSED IN THE STATE OF KANSAS."

The penny dropped.

In January of 2020 our law firm had been contacted by a rival firm in Buffalo. Their real estate litigator had fallen ill and they were about to commence a trial in Wichita. I had recently handled a very similar case in Buffalo and they hired me as their agent to assist them in the Wichita trial. Strings were pulled and dues were paid to make me a duly qualified lawyer in the state of Kansas. A few simple business cards were printed from our computer just in case they were needed while I was in Wichita.

On the day before we were flying out to Kansas, the parties settled the case so I never made the trip.

I got on the internet and located the phone number for the Kansas State Bar Association.

The lady I spoke with confirmed that I was still a duly paid-up member in good standing of the Kansas legal bar. The renewal applications for the 2021 memberships wouldn't be sent out until at least February because the coronavirus restrictions had delayed everything.

I was ecstatic when the call ended.

Carl Saunders could still practice law if he didn't mind moving to the state of Kansas.

That fortuitous discovery also meant that I could get out of the big city rat race and reside in a much smaller town.

Suddenly I was motivated to get my sorry ass out of New York State as quickly as possible.

I got back on my old desktop computer and prepared a notice to vacate my apartment effective next Saturday.

After delivering it personally to the superintendent along with my final rent check, I deposited the buy-out bank draft into my checking account.

At Wal-Mart I purchased some boxes and tape along with a road atlas showing each state in the USA on a separate page.

I cancelled my land line phone as well as the cable TV and internet service. Utilities were included in my rent so there was nothing I needed to do in that regard.

Back at the apartment I began packing up my belongings.

Although it was tempting to give away some of my clothes, in reality everything I owned could easily fit into my 2015 Hyundai Santa Fe SUV.

It was tempting to leave Buffalo today but instead I decided to wait until tomorrow. Tonight I could study the road atlas and choose a tentative route to Kansas.

Also I could eat up most of the food in my fridge. My freezer was empty except for ice cubes. I ate so many of my meals at the office or at restaurants that frozen dinners were a rarity for me.

My celebratory supper consisted of a huge salad in order to use up all my vegetables and salad dressing, washed down with several glasses of milk.

I left a bit of orange juice and just enough milk to cover my cereal tomorrow morning.

On Saturday morning after breakfast I packed my stuff into my vehicle, handed in my condo keys to the superintendent and pulled out of the parking lot at ten o'clock.

Carl Saunders, like so many other folks this year, was escaping New York State and its overly restrictive approach to the coronavirus.

About an hour later I was entering Pennsylvania just south of Jamestown on Highway 62.

The freedom I was suddenly feeling was quite exhilarating. This surprise late-life adventure was definitely something to anticipate with enthusiasm.

My new life had begun.

CHAPTER 4 (On the Road)

I was incredibly upbeat.

The weather was sunny and reasonably mild for the middle of December.

Strangely, no one would be able to contact me. I had used the firm smart phone as my personal cell phone which meant that I no longer had any phone whatsoever. My old personal email address wasn't transferable so Carl Saunders was suddenly a phantom.

That fact didn't upset me.

In fact it made me determined to start a new life in Kansas without any ties at all to Buffalo.

By twelve-thirty I was driving through Oil City enjoying the scenery and devising ways of preventing any vestiges of my New York life to follow me into Kansas.

It hadn't been necessary to provide anyone with my destination. That meant that no one on the planet had any idea where Carl Saunders was at this moment or where he was headed.

A brainwave hit me as I navigated some smaller highways to avoid driving through Youngstown, Ohio.

My name on the law firm's letterhead was simply Carl Saunders. I didn't use D. Carl Saunders or Donald Carl

Saunders on any accounts and hadn't displayed my law school or university diplomas on my office wall.

It was doubtful that anyone in the firm even realized that Carl was my middle name.

From now on I would become Donald Saunders and omit my middle name from all records.

That step would go a long way to permitting complete anonymity in Kansas.

By four o'clock I was entering the small city of Findlay, Ohio on Highway 224.

I spotted some chain hotels near the intersection with Interstate 75 and found a room for the night.

While I was relaxing before supper, I looked over the road atlas and felt that it was wise to head a bit further south tomorrow in order to avoid possible snowstorms.

I ate a nice supper at a restaurant right beside my hotel and then returned to my room where I studied the Kansas page in the road atlas.

The western half of the state was very sparsely populated. I definitely wanted to avoid Wichita, Topeka and Metropolitan Kansas City, the most populous cities.

That evaluation prompted me to focus on the southeast corner of Kansas and select Fort Scott, Pittsburg, Independence or Coffeyville as my new home.

Of those four small cities, Pittsburg was the largest with a population of roughly 20,000.

I pondered what I was looking for in my new home and decided that the other three cities in that area of the state were just a bit too small.

Having a specific destination infused me with a sense of purpose.

On Sunday the weather had turned a bit threatening although it wasn't snowing or raining.

I had coffee and donuts in the hotel lobby and then hit the road just before eight o'clock.

Two hours later I entered Indiana and kept driving, stopping only for gas and washroom breaks.

At one o'clock I entered Illinois where I veered south on Highway 1. I drove through a very pretty city called Danville and continued all the way to Norris City where I caught Highway 45.

The weather still hadn't turned nasty so I kept driving until after dark and finally reached Cape Girardeau, Missouri where I got a hotel room at a Super 8.

For supper I ate a submarine sandwich I had purchased when I filled up with gas at Harrisburg, Indiana.

It was roughly 370 miles from my hotel to Pittsburg, Kansas. I expected to reach my ultimate destination late tomorrow afternoon unless I hit a nasty winter storm.

On Monday morning I woke early. This motel didn't offer any food so I began driving at seven-thirty. There weren't many options so I took Highway 25 southwest until it intersected with Highway 60 which I followed all the way past Springfield.

At that point I veered north and caught Highway 126 into Pittsburg, Kansas. I had stopped for gas and a washroom break just once and had skipped breakfast and lunch altogether.

I drove around Pittsburg first. It was two o'clock in the afternoon and I found a nicely situated older motel called the Holiday Lodge which I booked for two nights.

I had arrived at my new home town.

CHAPTER 5 (House Purchase)

After checking in I drove around the town again and purchased a street map and a local newspaper.

There was a state university in Pittsburg and that made rental accommodation scarce. The classified section of the paper only listed two apartments and they were unusually expensive. I drove past the listed addresses but disliked the locations.

I drove around the commercial area of Pittsburg, parked near a real estate office and wandered inside.

Since I was awash in cash, it seemed logical to purchase a modest home rather than overpay for an apartment.

The office was quiet but an older gentleman wandered into the reception area, introduced himself as Pete Conrad and asked if he could assist me.

"I'm interested in taking a peek at what homes your agency has listed right now. While I'm here perhaps you could let me know what office space is currently for rent."

Pete had me sit in front of the reception area computer while he opened their listing website and instructed me how to use it to view the individual listings.

They weren't in any particular order.

We started with office space. Although there were many places for rent, the monthly cost seemed prohibitive given the difficulty I'd likely face in generating any profit. Running a small law office was going to be my hobby rather than being designed to provide me with income.

I was already wealthy.

Filling my time as a small town attorney was now my goal. It had stung to be shunted out of the legal profession by back-stabbing partners.

"The office space seems a bit too pricey so let's turn our attention to houses. I'm especially interested in a home with a bit of extra parking space and one which would be suitable for me to operate an office in addition to residing there."

"I don't think we have any listings like that. The city zoning does permit owners to run a home business out of their residence."

"In that case perhaps I'll concentrate on a house with some parking and a layout which lends itself to a side entrance into a separate room."

I flipped through the listings, many of which didn't even have a driveway.

One house was attractive both in design and price.

I asked the sales chap about it.

"That's been for sale since July. The owners moved out of the area when the wife found a better job in Coffeyville. It's been vacant since the middle of September although they've left some furniture in order to make the place more attractive."

"Why isn't it selling?"

"The décor is hideous. Every room has garish paint or horridly outdated wallpaper and carpet. As you look at the photos you'll soon notice that every room sports a different color. Most buyers today want open concept and move-in ready condition with a neutral color scheme. This place screams that's it's horribly outdated."

"The price seems quite reasonable."

"It's not if you consider the major renovations that would be required to modernize that house."

"Are there any structural problems with the building?"

"No. In fact they obtained a professional building inspection report at the time they listed the place. There's a copy of it in our file. The only problems are the outrageous color scheme and the old-fashioned layout."

Pete left to grab the listing file. He returned and handed me the inspection report. It disclosed a couple of minor flaws but Pete mentioned that they had already been repaired.

"Do you think the vendors would be motivated to drop their price with a very quick closing date?"

"I can take you through the place right now if you've got the time."

I was agreeable so we drove to the property at 210 Church Street.

This was a two-storey wooden home surrounded by a white picket fence. There was a reasonably wide driveway leading to a detached garage at the rear of the lot.

The listing showed that the home was constructed in 1920 and had gas heat. A new roof had been installed in 2016 and the electrical panel had been upgraded to 200-Amp service in 2018.

There were three bedrooms and a bathroom upstairs while the main floor contained a living-room, a spacious separate dining-room, the kitchen and another bathroom.

The main front entrance led into the living-room area while a side door led from the driveway into the dining-room.

The basement was completely unfinished but contained the furnace and electrical panel.

As a testament to the fact that most attorneys had no taste, I actually loved the loud colors throughout the home as I walked from room to room.

Of particular appeal to me was the ease with which I could employ the dining-room with its separate side entrance as my legal office.

"I'm willing to submit an offer for $45,000 with all existing furniture included. I'll pay my own closing costs and insert a clause that I'm buying the place in 'as is' condition. I'll even close the deal this Thursday if they accept my terms without any changes."

"That won't give you enough time to obtain financing."

"I'll be paying cash."

The agent couldn't get me back to the office fast enough. The actual listing agent, Sharon Courtland had arrived in the office while we were out so Pete brought her in to meet me.

Pete explained the terms of my offer. Sharon decided that it would save time if she phoned her clients immediately before the offer was prepared.

Sharon reached the owners and told them the tentative terms of the offer, wisely emphasizing the positive aspects before hitting them with the low price.

When asked, I responded that my price was firm. It was a take it or leave it situation.

Sharon took her phone into the next room. Since she was wearing a face mask, she unconsciously spoke more loudly than normal which meant that Pete and I could hear every word.

It was a tough sell but Sharon agreed to drop the realty commission by $1,000 and that sealed the deal.

The offer was prepared. I signed it and Sharon emailed it to her clients who accepted the terms. I paid a cash deposit of $1,000 to the realtor.

The sellers phoned their attorney in Coffeyville who advised that she could accommodate the rapid closing date.

Pete called a local real estate lawyer named Darlene Allems who also confirmed that she could be ready for a Thursday morning closing.

I drove to my lawyer's office before she closed up for the day and provided her with whatever information she required.

Tomorrow I would arrange to have $46,000 wired to her trust account from my bank which would likely be enough to cover the balance of the purchase price and the closing costs.

I would also arrange homeowner's insurance and contact the utility companies.

I still hadn't eaten yet today.

I booked my motel room for Wednesday night and then walked to a nearby restaurant where I feasted on a small pizza and two large mugs of draft beer.

It had only taken me a few hours to find permanent accommodation in Pittsburg and at a great bargain.

That was an excellent omen.

CHAPTER 6 (Surrounded by Color)

Strangely enough, I had no misgivings about my rash decision to purchase a home without even determining first whether I would like Pittsburg as a place to live.

Residing in my new house would be much cheaper than renting an apartment. Despite my wealth, I was a very frugal individual, much to the disgust of my former partners, all of whom drove expensive automobiles and resided in lavish homes. Come to think about it, my ex-wife never appreciated my love affair with thrift either.

I slept long and well although the three long days of driving likely had a lot to do with it.

On Tuesday I attended at a local branch of my bank and transferred all my accounts there. By doing so it also made it much easier to get the purchase funds to my attorney. My new Pittsburg bank branch prepared a bank draft payable to Darlene Allems in trust and I delivered the draft to Darlene.

While at the bank I also changed the name of my accounts from Carl Saunders to Donald Saunders which was surprisingly easy to do since my identification documents showed my full name.

Insurance was easy to arrange and I added a rider on my homeowner's policy to show that I would be operating a home business from the property.

I was amazed at how open for business it was here in Kansas. Although I wore masks whenever I was indoors anywhere, businesses were open.

Even the utility companies and the municipal tax office were open for business so I was able to sign whatever documents were required in order to have the billings switched into the name of Donald Saunders.

Once the house purchase actually closed, then I'd be able to obtain a telephone line as well as internet and cable TV service.

A snowstorm hit early on Wednesday which kept me close to the motel all day. I did walk through the snow to the nearest restaurant for breakfast and supper.

By Thursday morning the roads were plowed and the sun was shining.

Since this was the day before Christmas, I dropped in to my lawyer's office at eleven o'clock. Darlene had just returned from the land registry office in the county seat of Girard about twelve miles to the northwest where she had completed the real estate transaction.

She handed me the keys and advised that her office was closing today at noon but that I could pick up my report letter and accompanying documents next Tuesday.

I drove to my new home at 210 Church Street and carried my car-load of belongings inside.

Then I found a pay phone and called a company which could provide phone, cable TV and internet service for one bundled price.

The sales representative advised that the service would be hooked up remotely within three hours.

In the afternoon I examined my new digs and made a list of items I'd need to purchase, one of which was a vacuum cleaner.

The furniture left in the house was extensive enough. The sellers had left the dining-room virtually empty but that suited me because it would become my legal office.

They had left a sofa and chair in the living-room along with a coffee table and a lamp table.

There was a small table and two chairs in the kitchen and the old fridge and stove seemed to be in good working order.

Two of the upstairs bedrooms were completely empty but the biggest bedroom contained a full bedroom set.

Pete Conrad's derogatory comments about the garish color scheme made me chuckle.

I adored the vibrant colors and didn't intend to change a thing.

The living-room walls were bright red to match the carpet.

The dining-room sported a deep purple carpet with matching ceiling paint and the walls were wallpapered with intricate designs incorporating every shade of purple imaginable. I wondered what my clients would think of the décor.

A professional designer would perhaps grade my soon-to-be office as "country bumpkin."

The upstairs bedrooms were respectively dark green, bright blue and brilliant yellow.

I loved the yellow room which happened to be the largest of the three bedrooms and the one I intended to use myself.

Before the grocery stores closed, I whipped out and bought various food items to sustain me over the Christmas holiday and beyond.

The three hour promise wasn't kept but just before I went to bed, my phone and internet were up and running. I didn't have a television set but would probably purchase one next week.

I was too tired to surf the internet but I did manage to set up a new email address for my office and for my personal use.

I felt as if Santa Claus had already given me my Christmas gift, namely freedom from the Buffalo rat race.

CHAPTER 7 (Quiet Christmas Break)

I woke up on Christmas morning to a blaze of yellow. The sun was streaming in my bedroom window and illuminating a surround-sound of multiple shades of yellow.

I found it exceedingly cheerful.

Another remarkable change was in my attitude. I was no longer miffed with my former law partners for kicking me out of the firm.

In actual fact they had done me an immense favor.

Freedom was exhilarating.

After breakfast I got on my computer and began my education about Pittsburg, the local legal bar and areas in which Kansas laws were different from the New York system.

That endeavor kept me busy all day.

In fact I accessed the Kansas State Law Association website and watched several educational videos regarding real estate law, business law and insurance law.

Over the next few days I did the preliminary work necessary before I opened my home office.

I purchased a lovely antique desk and matching bookcase from the widow of an elderly lawyer.

I also ordered business cards as well as a sign for my side door and another for my front lawn.

In order to comply with the home occupation rules of Pittsburg, I couldn't use the term "LAW OFFICE" but I could display my name "DONALD SAUNDERS" with the words "ATTORNEY-AT-LAW" or just "LAWYER" underneath my name.

There was no restriction for my business cards which could show my address and phone number.

It would have been a hassle persuading the phone company to install a separate business telephone number because they had a rule prohibiting business lines in a residence.

However, that didn't bother me because I was happy to use my new land line home number as my office phone number as well. For one thing it saved me money. Also, I doubted that I'd ever be busy enough for a separate line anyway.

My law office was to be my hobby, not my career.

I purchased various office paper and supplies as well as a photocopier.

I also opened a business account and a trust account at a local credit union whose office was just three short blocks from my home.

Obtaining negligence insurance, joining the county bar association and completing a few on-line continuing education courses were the final tasks before opening my office, and I had those items duly completed by the last day of 2020.

My "office" signs and business cards were ready for pick-up on Thursday, the 30th of December. I picked them up but didn't hang out the lawn sign or the sign on my side door until Friday, the first day of 2021.

Finally on Monday, the 4th of January I unlocked my office door and was ready for business.

I had taken out an advertisement in the local newspaper announcing the establishment of my law office and that ad would run continuously for three consecutive days commencing on January 5th.

CHAPTER 8 (One Solitary Client)

By Thursday I was getting increasingly bored.

Rather than being uncomfortable in a suit and tie, on Wednesday I had decided to dress casually.

My phone hadn't rung even once and sitting around all day waiting for clients was very uninspiring.

I regretted having spent $294 for the newspaper announcement.

At least I'd had plenty of time to reflect about my future.

Some clarity had appeared.

Although being a small town lawyer had long ago been a dream of mine, I now felt that handling residential real estate transactions and small claims disputes were beneath a top-notch litigation attorney with forty-two years under his belt.

At first I might take on whichever clients wandered in the door or called me on the phone, but even that was doubtful.

Assisting folks with their mundane problems didn't appear to be my cup of tea at this late stage of my career.

Donald Saunders, formerly known as Carl Saunders, craved more of a challenge but it was unlikely that any interesting files would come my way until I had proven to my legal rivals here in Pittsburg that I was highly competent.

As so often happened with know-it-all attorneys, I was completely wrong.

Shortly after lunch on Thursday a poorly dressed couple knocked on my side door and entered the office. They were quite frail and both of them could barely walk.

I stood up, introduced myself and asked how I could assist them.

They were wearing masks so I pulled my own out of a desk drawer and put it on.

"We've got a real serious problem," the man rasped as he fiddled with his mask.

"Please sit down and tell me what the trouble is," I responded.

"Damn these masks. I'm itching like crazy and I want to see who I'm dealing with."

"I can't stand them either. Tell you what. Don't snitch on me to the authorities and we can all remove our face masks."

"It's a deal," the man barked as he ripped his mask off. His wife did the same only more gently. I took my own mask off and placed it back in the drawer.

"You're not from around here, are you?" the lady inquired.

"I'm not. I just moved to Pittsburg a few days before Christmas."

"Are you really a lawyer?" the chap asked. "This is the strangest looking office I've ever seen and you're dressed like you're going to repair your truck."

"Mind your manners, Harold," his wife admonished.

"Yes I am a qualified attorney despite my lack of a suit and tie. This tiny office is my retirement hobby and you're my first potential clients."

"We don't have a plug nickel to pay you with," Harold confessed.

"That's a shame. Does this mean I'll lose my deposit on that new Mercedes Benz I've had my eye on?"

Harold laughed at my comment.

I decided that I liked the fellow.

"I've got an idea. Let's call this a free consultation. You can explain the legal problem you've got and I'll listen carefully and let you know whether I can help you or not. Please start by telling me your names."

"I'm Joan Els and this is my husband, Harold."

"It's nice to meet you, Joan and Harold. Now tell me all about your problem."

CHAPTER 9 (Tough Breaks)

Harold cleared his throat and began his explanation.

"We've got two serious problems but they're kind of linked up. Joan and I don't have any money coming in right now and that's put us way behind in our property taxes."

"Where is your home?"

"It's a mile west of Capaldo which is a tiny hamlet about five miles from here."

"Why don't you start right from the beginning so I can understand the full extent of your situation?"

Harold looked uncomfortable. In fact I thought he was going to cry.

Joan took over.

"Our troubles began three years ago this month. Our only child got himself in some serious legal trouble back then and hired a big-shot lawyer from Wichita to defend him. Harold and I didn't have any savings. It's always been a struggle and money's always real tight. The lawyer took a mortgage on our property in case our son lost the case."

"What was the case about?"

"We're not really sure. Dexter was accused of swindling some folks in

Wichita. They sued him for the money they lost and the Sheriff there charged Dexter with theft."

"Where is Dexter now?"

"He's in prison up in Lawrence."

"I take it that he was found guilty."

"That's right. The folks who made the complaint dropped the lawsuit when they discovered that Dexter was flat broke but he was sentenced to six years by the judge."

"I understand. Tell me what happened next."

"About a year later Harold got injured while he was up on a ladder fixing a roof. Harold was a self-employed general all-around handyman. We had insurance to cover his lost income and made the claim on our policy. That was almost two years ago. We've gotten nothing but the run-around from the company and they haven't paid us a cent so far."

"I take it that you're thinking of hiring me to battle it out with your insurance company over payment of the claim."

"That's just a part of our problem."

"What's the rest of the story?"

"The lawyer who holds our mortgage had been real patient with us because he knew we were waiting for the insurance money, but in October he sold the mortgage to a neighbor of ours named Johnathan Baxter. Baxter owns the land all around us and has wanted to buy us out for many years. He's incredibly rich. Now it looks like he's going to get his wish."

Joan pulled some papers out of her purse and handed them over to me.

It was a bit confusing but I concluded that the lawyer was no longer involved in the picture.

Johnathan Baxter was calling in his mortgage.

The demand for payment had been served on the Els twenty-eight days ago which meant that they had until Saturday to come up with the money.

I read the original mortgage document. It had been a simple demand mortgage in the principal amount of $17,000 bearing no interest and not repayable until thirty days after a written demand had been served on the borrowers.

"I see why you're so frantic. There's no way your insurance company would pay you enough policy proceeds by Saturday. They've already been giving you the runaround for almost two years."

"There's more to the fix we're in," Harold admitted.

"I'm listening."

"As I said earlier, we're behind on our property taxes. The county is going to sell our home by a tax sale if we don't pay up the arrears by the end of this month."

"Is that it or is there still more?"

"That's the pickle we're in," Joan moaned.

"Why are you waiting until the last minute to consult an attorney?"

"You're our last hope," Joan responded. "We've contacted every other lawyer in Pittsburg and most of the firms in Coffeyville. Nobody around here wants to do battle with Johnathan Baxter. We saw your ad in the Pittsburg newspaper and figured that since you're a stranger to these parts, then you might be able to help us."

"What will you do if Baxter forecloses on you or if the county sells your place at a tax sale?"

"We've got no relatives or friends. I guess we'll live in our beat-up old pick-up truck until we're both dead from exposure."

"Don't you collect social security?"

"We ain't old enough," Harold replied.

I felt guilty that I had inadvertently insulted them but they looked much older than me.

"How have you managed to pay your utilities or your house insurance?"

"Our hydro was cut off a year ago. We've been heating the place with wood. We haven't had insurance for almost two years."

"Haven't you bought groceries?"

"We've been living on vegetables in the nice weather and bottled preserves in the winter. We've always grown our own food."

"Haven't you applied for welfare?"

Harold snapped the reply.

"We're not deadbeats. We're just simple country folk who sometimes trust what people tell us. The guy who sold us the income protection insurance told us if I got injured or sick, the company would look after us proper."

"How much do you think your property is worth?"

Joan fielded that question.

"We had a realtor fellow come by last summer. He told us our home isn't worth any more than $15,000 and only then if we fixed up a bunch of things. Harold can't even do simple repairs no more and my own health is worse than his. We've got no medical insurance either. If we get sick, we just grin and bear it."

"As I mentioned earlier, you're my first potential clients. If everyone around here is floundering in a mess as bad as yours, I might regret opening up this office as my new hobby."

Joan was close to tears as she made her final plea.

"Will you help us, Mr. Saunders?"

"I might just do that. Do you have anything from your insurance company to show me?"

Joan extracted another bundle of papers from her purse and shoved them across the desk.

I glanced at the correspondence, all of which was typical delaying tactics. Then I briefly read the policy itself.

When I was done, I leaned back in my chair and closed my eyes while I correlated everything I'd learned.

Finally I opened my eyes and smiled.

"I guess you've come to the right place. Yes, I'll sort out your problems."

CHAPTER 10 (Making My First Enemy)

I phoned my credit union and requested that they prepare two bank drafts, one payable to Johnathan Baxter's lawyer in trust for $17,150 representing the full payout balance of the mortgage plus the attorney's fee for preparing the discharge, and the other payable to the County of Crawford in the amount of $1,786.00 being the full amount of property tax arrears and penalty.

Then I addressed Mr. and Mrs. Els.

"I'm also going to loan you $1,064. Will that be enough to get your hydro hooked back up and enable you to buy groceries and place insurance on your home and pick-up truck?"

"Why would you do all that for us?"

"I'll prepare a simple demand promissory note in the amount of $20,000 which I'll have you sign now. That's the total of the funds I'm loaning you. Your most pressing problems will have been taken care of for the moment. Tomorrow we'll tackle your fight with the insurance company. I'll study your policy this evening."

I counted out $1,064 from my wallet and handed the cash to Joan. Then I banged off the promissory note and had them sign it. I also prepared a brief letter to Baxter's lawyer.

"Now I'll drive us to the credit union, then to the office of Baxter's lawyer which is here in town. Tomorrow I'll deliver your tax payment to the county tax office in Girard. Where is the utility company which looks after your hydro?"

"It's here in Pittsburg," Harold responded.

"Where is your insurance agent's office?"

"They're also here in town."

"We'll hit those offices too at the end of our delivery run."

The credit union had the two bank drafts ready by the time we arrived.

The lawyer's office was in a strip plaza in the north end of town.

Joan and Harold went in with me. They mentioned that the lawyer was Johnathan Baxter's brother-in-law.

The chap's name was Desmond Carlyle and he was definitely displeased when he read my letter and I handed him the bank draft.

He tried to refuse payment with a ridiculous reason he made up on the fly but I was adamant. Voices were raised but I refused to back down and threatened to launch a lawsuit against him if he didn't accept payment forthwith and provide me with the signed discharge. His demand letter to Mr. and Mrs. Els had specifically stated that he had the signed discharge in his file and that it would be exchanged for the payout money.

Desmond backed down but not without a not-so-subtle threat that I'd regret what I was doing.

I insisted on a receipt in addition to immediate possession of the signed discharge.

The other errands were non-contentious and didn't take long.

Finally I drove my clients back to my office. They drove off in their now properly insured vehicle.

Joan had hugged me tightly and Harold had shaken my hand vigorously just before they left.

We made an appointment for tomorrow at eleven o'clock at which time we could devise a strategy to force their insurance company to cough up all the money they owed under the policy. I told them to bring me their income tax returns for the past several years.

For the next hour I pored over the actual insurance policy and perused carefully the correspondence.

It seemed to me that the company hadn't formally denied coverage but had delayed any payment up to now on the basis that they were still investigating the claim.

Tomorrow I'd make my second enemy.

CHAPTER 11 (Insurance Sharks)

Strangely as I climbed into bed at ten o'clock, I had no regrets about spending more than $20,000 of my own funds to assist Harold and Joan.

In a way this was the type of situation I had envisaged in my daydreams over the decades that I would have handled if I had opened up my own law office at the beginning of my career rather than joining a law firm as soon as I had passed the New York State bar exams.

On Friday morning I drove to Girard where I registered the mortgage discharge at the land registry office.

The county tax office was in the same building so I paid Harold and Joan's tax arrears and obtained a proper receipt.

I was back in my office well before eleven o'clock.

Harold and Joan showed up on time at eleven o'clock, having obtained a renewal sticker for their vehicle's license plate before arriving.

The income tax returns showed Harold's self-employed earnings for each year from 2010 to 2018. His injury had occurred in February of 2019 and that ended his income stream. His gross income for 2019 was $2,100 all of which he had earned prior to his accident. He hadn't filed his 2020 income tax return yet but confirmed that he hadn't earned a dime because he was no longer able to work.

During the years prior to 2019 Harold's income fluctuated a bit but generally was in the $20,000 range annually.

Harold had purchased the income protection policy in 2015 and had paid the monthly premiums regularly until shortly after his accident at which time the insurance company notified him by letter that they were cancelling his policy and that there would be no further premiums deducted from his bank account.

"I believe that I've got a handle on the matter. I recommend that you leave the legal strategy completely up to me."

"That's fine with us," Harold replied. "We haven't got a clue how to make the company pay us the money they owe us."

"I'm going to prepare a retainer agreement. In it you will agree to repay the money I've loaned you from any insurance proceeds you receive. As far as my legal fee, I'll charge you either an hourly fee for the time I expend plus any disbursements I've had to pay out or a flat fee based on a percentage up to thirty percent of the amount you collect. Your bill will be the lower of those amounts."

"Does that mean that you'll wind up with our insurance money instead of us getting it?" Harold inquired.

"I'll confiscate some of it, that's for sure. My goal is to force the insurance company to pay you an amount equivalent to your average annual income from the day of your accident until you turn sixty-five. That's what the policy agrees to pay you. Since you're only sixty years of age, then the company should owe you about $135,000. If I charged you thirty percent of that amount and also repaid my loan, then I'd wind up with about $60,000 of your settlement and you'd get about $75,000."

"What if you can't squeeze one red cent out of them?" Joan queried.

"That would mean that I'm a dreadful lawyer and won't deserve a penny. I'd rip up your promissory note and would also lose any disbursements like court filing fees that I paid out on your behalf."

"That doesn't seem fair to you," Joan said.

"I doubt if you'd get such an attractive offer from any other attorney around here but you've got a solid legal case against the insurance company. If I get spanked by the Kansas legal system and lose the case, then I'm willing to accept my punishment."

"What's our next step?" Harold asked.

"You can go home and relax. Since you don't have a telephone, how can I contact you if I need to?"

"I'll give you my friend's phone number," Joan answered. "She can drive over to our place and give me the message."

"That's fine. Just so you know, I'm going to sue the insurance company today. At the very least that will show them that we're serious and should make them respond."

Before Joan and Harold left, I had them describe to me in detail the hardships they had to face because of the insurance company's failure to pay the claim promptly.

As soon as my clients left, I crafted a proper Statement of Claim and drove to Girard where I paid the filing fee and the cost of having the document duly served on the insurance company at their head office in Wichita.

I was itching for a battle.

Rubbing the insurance sharks' noses in their own feces would be hugely satisfying.

CHAPTER 12 (First Contact)

The weekend passed pleasantly. I studied up on Kansas insurance law which really was virtually identical to that of New York State.

In the lawsuit I had claimed $135,250 for the lump sum payment from the date of Harold's accident until he turned sixty-five, and I had also added a claim for an additional $300,000 to compensate Harold for the pain and suffering he had been forced to endure because of the insurance company's failure to honor the terms of their policy.

I had given a lot of thought to the situation and decided that actually going to court in front of a judge or jury would maximize the award.

However, that would also delay actual payment of any funds for at least a couple of years and even longer if the company appealed the verdict.

From long experience I suspected that this company would need to be humiliated on a motion or two before it began to talk turkey.

This country bumpkin was just the guy to administer the harsh lesson that appearances can be deceiving.

The first contact from the insurance company occurred on Tuesday morning when I received a phone call from an attorney named Dwayne Rackham who was employed by a legal firm in Wichita.

The chap, who appeared to be rather young based on his voice, requested a face to face meeting this week to discuss the file.

It seemed a very unusual request since Rackham worked out of Wichita until he mentioned that he was commencing a trial in the Crawford County seat of Girard on Thursday morning.

We settled on Wednesday at one o'clock which would allow sufficient time for the drive from Wichita. Rackham would attend at my office with another member of his law firm.

"We haven't had the pleasure of dealing with you before, Mr. Saunders. How long have you been in practice?"

"I've only had my office up and running since Monday but next month I'll reach my first anniversary as an attorney in Kansas."

I purposely omitted that I had practised top-level litigation for forty-two years in New York State.

There was a reason for that deception.

Rackham was likely setting up the meeting for the sole purpose of evaluating his opponent. He wasn't coming to Pittsburg to discuss settlement negotiations. His client would have Rackham attempt first to thoroughly intimidate me.

Sure enough, shortly after we ended the call, I received an email confirming tomorrow's meeting from the law firm on their full letterhead which listed fifty-seven attorneys.

I looked them up on the internet and learned that Dwayne Rackham wasn't a youngster after all. He had been called to the Kansas legal bar in 2001 and was already a full partner in the firm.

His profile listed some of the reported cases he had handled and I studied the decisions in each of the ones mentioned. Not surprisingly, Rackham had been victorious in those cases. Firms didn't bother to publicize the battles they lost.

I spent Tuesday evening drafting a thorough chronology of the hardships that Harold and his wife had endured. It was actually quite compelling and made my blood boil that the insurance company had opted to screw their clients around rather than pay a legitimate claim.

In fact the reason I had used my veto power to reject the new insurance company client at my old firm was that I would have felt too unclean assisting

the vultures in shafting their most vulnerable clients.

CHAPTER 13 (Hick Lawyer)

On Wednesday my first decision after breakfast was whether to wear a suit and tie or dress casually.

I opted for the hick look.

My hair was mostly snow white with some remaining grey which suggested that I was a kindly old gentleman.

I purposely refrained from combing my hair this morning in order to appear somewhat like the mad professor, and I dressed in a long-sleeve yellow sweatshirt and blue jeans, both of which were still somewhat rumpled from the long car journey. White socks and white running shoes completed my ensemble.

I purposely fried up a bacon sandwich for lunch so that my office would smell like a greasy diner to my pending guests.

Promptly at one o'clock my adversaries knocked on my dining-room door. I yelled for them to come on in.

It was obvious from their crinkled noses and wide-open eyes that my bacon fry-up combined with the visual onslaught of purple was almost too much for them to absorb.

In all three people entered.

I recognized Rackham from his firm photo and he was the first to enter. Directly behind him were two extremely attractive ladies.

They were rendered speechless but nevertheless I continued with the rube attorney façade.

"Oh my goodness, there are three of you. I only have two office chairs. Let me go grab one of my kitchen chairs."

As I exited the office I purposely left the French doors between it and the living-room open. I wanted my opponents to be assaulted by the bright red carpets and walls in the room opposite the hallway.

The hallway was itself quite colorful with bright green carpet and wall-papered walls containing varying shades of green.

I brought one of my rather ratty kitchen chairs into the room.

"I can't ask either of you lovely ladies to sit on this filthy chair. I'll use it myself."

With that concession, I wheeled my own office chair around my desk and into an empty space near the two client chairs.

"Now that the setting has been altered to accommodate a larger crowd than anticipated, please let me introduce myself. I'm Donald Saunders."

Rackham did the honors.

"It's nice to meet you, Donald. I'm Dwayne Rackham and this is my associate Arlene Fawcett and my legal assistant Tammy Mick."

We all shook hands after which I walked around to my kitchen chair.

"Please take a seat and we can get down to business," I insisted.

Rackham took charge.

"We've had an opportunity to peruse your statement of claim and discuss the file with the adjuster and his supervisor. Your clients' claim was being processed. Why did you not contact the adjuster directly first and discuss the progress of the matter? It wasn't necessary to sue the company without even speaking with them."

"I examined the correspondence. Mr. and Mrs. Els are my very first clients and I felt it prudent to grab the insurance company's attention immediately. Harold and Joan are too polite and unsophisticated to realize that they were getting the runaround from their insurance company."

"It's an enormously complex claim," Rackham retorted.

"It looked pretty simple to me."

"We've taken the liberty of preparing both a Statement of Defence and a Motion to dismiss the claim. We've just filed both documents at the court house in Girard before we continued here to Pittsburg. Will you accept service of these documents?"

"Can I look at them first?"

"Of course you can, Donald."

Tammy extracted some papers from her briefcase and handed them to me.

The Statement of Defence was strictly boiler-plate meaning that it lacked any specifics. The Motion was no better. This was a common practice. Keep your best evidence hidden for as long as possible.

"Where do you want me to sign?"

I knew precisely where my signatures needed to be but I still wanted to portray the aura of ineptitude.

I executed the documents and was handed my own copies.

The Motion would be heard on Friday afternoon in Girard.

"I notice that you're seeking costs of the Motion. May I inquire as to the estimated amount of those costs?"

Arlene Fawcett replied that their legal account was expected to be in the $5,000 range.

"That's acceptable. My own account will match that figure in the event that the Judge dismisses your Motion. Are we agreed on that cost figure?"

Dwayne Rackham at that moment turned on the charm.

"At least we do agree on the level of costs. That's a reasonable start.

Look, Donald, this matter doesn't need to become a nasty confrontation. Our law firm rarely loses a case. Please be a bit more realistic. A sole practitioner in a small town has little chance of a positive verdict when he is up against a huge Wichita law firm representing a wealthy insurance company."

"The odds do seem stacked against my clients but they have suffered enormously because of your client's unconscionable delay in processing the claim. Please read the summary I've provided you of the specific hardships that my clients have endured."

Rackham's big-city arrogance shone through.

"I don't need to read it. Facts don't matter. You're going to lose the case even if the Motion to dismiss is denied but you can avoid that embarrassment and earn a fee at the same time. We're prepared to offer your clients $12,000 and absorb our legal costs."

I felt a bit naughty.

I opened my desk drawer and pulled out my calculator.

"That would only get me $3,600 for my fee. I can earn more than that simply by winning Friday's Motion. I'm sorry but I can't accept your offer."

"Shouldn't you run the offer by your clients first?" Arlene inquired.

"I don't need to. They've given me total authority to negotiate."

"How much would persuade you to settle the case?"

"The main claim for $135,250 is non-negotiable. As far as the damages for pain and suffering, I'm willing to start the bidding at $75,000."

Rackham burst out laughing.

"We'll see you on Friday, Donald. Please don't take offense but you're out of your mind."

"I get that a lot, Dwayne. Make sure you've got your check book with you on Friday. And by the way, Arlene, read the summary of the ordeal your client put Joan and Harold through. Dwayne's dismissive attitude just upped my best offer to $100,000."

The attitude immediately turned hostile.

Rackham stood up and his team copied him.

"You're going to learn a bitter lesson, Saunders. The big boys don't play nice."

"My offer might not seem so outrageous on Friday while you're writing the check to cover my costs on the Motion, Dwayne. I'm sure that even someone with your oratorical skills must realize that some cases win themselves. Read the paper I gave you before you try to feed me your bullshit stew."

Rackham's face turned beet red with rage but he kept his lip zipped and they left the office.

We had all broken the Covid-19 rules by not wearing face masks.

Astute attorneys realized that they needed to evaluate facial expressions in order to maximize understanding of their opponents.

Face masks turned human beings into emotionless robots.

CHAPTER 14 (Negative Opinion)

Dwayne Rackham waited until the others were in the car and he had backed out of the driveway before speaking.

"Can you believe that idiot? He's the most incompetent boob I've ever come across."

"I thought I was going to puke all over my briefcase," Arlene retorted. "I don't think I'll ever eat bacon again."

That elicited a hearty laugh from all three occupants.

Even Tammy Mick joined the fun.

"I so wanted to ask Mr. Saunders for the name of his decorator."

"I just know I'm going to have nightmares about being thrown into a purple prison," Arlene quipped.

Rackham responded.

"That's nothing compared to the hideous green in the hallway or the red monstrosity that I suppose he calls his living-room. I wonder if he uses the rest of the house as a brothel."

Arlene answered.

"I'm surprised his phone didn't ring while we were there. Hi, this is Billy-Bob. Can I rent Bambi in the red room for a hundred bucks an hour at eight o'clock tonight?"

They all laughed.

"It's going to be fun rubbing his face in the dirt," Rackham declared. "I hope he's wearing that wrinkly yellow sweatshirt when he shows up for the Motion on Friday."

There were no decent hotels in Girard so the team was staying in suites at an upscale hotel chain in Pittsburg.

They arrived at their hotel within a few minutes and checked into their rooms.

Rackham gave instructions to his legal assistant.

"Find out what you can about Donald Saunders on the internet, Tammy and report back to me. I'm going to work on my opening remarks for tomorrow's trial."

Tammy tried for an hour to find information about the strange attorney they had just met but came up virtually empty.

Saunders was a member of the Kansas Bar Association but had only joined in 2020. She couldn't find out anything else.

Tammy phoned Dwayne's room and informed him of her lack of success.

Arlene relaxed on her bed and pulled out the paper that Donald Saunders had referred to.

She began reading and was quickly horrified at the abject poverty Mr. and Mrs. Els had endured within weeks of Harold's accident.

The poor couple had lived without hydro and without groceries. They had survived on vegetables from their own garden and bottled preserves from their basement.

Arlene knocked on Dwayne's door and handed him the summary which Saunders had prepared.

"You should read this, Dwayne. Our client really put these poor folks through the wringer. Saunders has a pretty compelling case if his description is even remotely accurate."

"I'll glance at it if I have the time, Arlene. Right now I need to finish my opening statement for my trial. I'm going to get room service for supper and I'll meet you and Tammy for breakfast in the hotel restaurant tomorrow morning at seven-thirty. Goodnight."

Thursday was taken up solely with the trial which thankfully wrapped up at six o'clock with a settlement.

That meant that on Friday morning Rackham could handle the execution of the settlement documents while Arlene could deal with the Saunders Motion at ten o'clock and then they would all drive immediately back to Wichita.

CHAPTER 15 (Easy Money)

Thursday was quiet in the office. The phone only rang twice and both times were telemarketers. It hadn't taken them long to find me.

On Friday I dressed in an expensive black pin-stripe suit and drove to Girard.

Arlene Fawcett arrived while I was sitting in the Judge's waiting room wearing my face mask. Arlene didn't recognize me because of the suit and face mask. She therefore totally ignored me which was fine with me.

Judge Jane Plowright opened the door to her chambers.

"Are you folks here for the ten o'clock Motion?"

"I'm Arlene Fawcett representing the defendant, Judge but Donald Saunders hasn't arrived yet. He's the attorney for the plaintiffs."

I had already risen to my feet when the Judge poked her head into the waiting room.

"I'm Donald Saunders on behalf of Harold and Joan Els."

"Excellent. Please come in to my chambers and we can get started."

I allowed Arlene to proceed first and I closed the waiting room door behind me.

"I'm Judge Plowright. This room is large enough to permit social distancing. With everyone's permission we can remove our face masks."

Hearing no objections, the Judge ripped off her mask. Arlene and I did the same.

"Ms. Fawcett, you initiated this Motion. Why do you want me to dismiss the plaintiffs' claim at this very preliminary stage?"

Arlene tried her best to make a compelling argument but the facts were not in her favor in any respect of the proceeding.

"Thank you, Ms. Fawcett. I see that you're with the same law firm based in Wichita which appeared yesterday on another claim against the same defendant as this one."

"That's correct, Judge. Our firm handles a large volume of defence work on behalf of various insurance companies."

"I see. Mr. Saunders, where are you from?"

"I've recently established my own legal practice in the nearby city of Pittsburg."

"That's interesting. Welcome to Crawford County. Please explain why I should deny Ms. Fawcett's Motion."

I began by referring to the Statement of Claim which laid out the delay tactics of the insurance company.

"Just in case the defendant had naughty intentions of letting the limitation period expire and using the lapse of time as a successful defence, I commenced legal action. The Statement of Defence filed by the insurance company contains little in the way of specific information regarding their possible denial of my clients' claim, but please permit me to quickly lay out some of the legal issues which will need to be determined at trial."

For the next few minutes I referred to the correspondence from the insurance company which simply indicated that the claim was still being investigated and I also enumerated the dreadful poverty into which my clients had fallen because of the unconscionable delay.

Finally I picked apart one by one the various reasons for dismissal cited by Arlene.

"Ms. Fawcett's firm and I on Wednesday in my office failed in our initial attempt to settle this matter but we did agree that the costs of the winning party today were to be $5,000. Isn't that correct, Ms. Fawcett?"

"That was the figure that was bandied about but there was no actual agreement."

"I am getting older, Ms. Fawcett and my memory might be slightly faulty but I distinctly heard your boss Dwayne Rackham state that at least we agreed on the level of costs of this Motion even if we were far apart on the lawsuit settlement itself. Is that not correct?"

"Mr. Rackham did say that," Arlene admitted reluctantly.

"Then the issue of costs is settled so that Judge Plowright doesn't have to set an amount herself. I've brought my check book in case your Motion is approved by the Judge. I do hope that you've done the same in case your Motion is denied."

Judge Plowright seemed to be greatly enjoying this exchange. She appeared to be in her fifties and was no doubt well aware of the slimy tactics practised by insurance companies and their attorneys.

I had looked up the Judge's history on the internet and discovered that she had been a litigator specializing in motor vehicle accidents for much of her career until she ascended to the bench.

"Are there any additional arguments that either attorney wishes to make?" the Judge inquired.

Arlene and I both responded in the negative.

"In that case I hereby deny defendant's Motion with costs. Plaintiff's counsel has easily persuaded me that the claim has potential legitimacy and that it would be a travesty of justice to dismiss the claim before discoveries have even taken place. As counsel have already agreed, the costs of this Motion are set at $5,000 and I hereby order that said cost award be paid immediately to plaintiff's counsel."

We thanked the Judge who left the chambers and went into her office.

Arlene glared at me as she wrote the check to me in trust and handed it to me.

"That was downright mean of you to set us up like that at your office. You came across as an incompetent buffoon. Believe me, we'll be fully ready for you in the future."

"Your client has horribly shafted Harold and Joan Els and your boss tried to take advantage of what he perceived to be my inexperience at our meeting on Wednesday. Rackham knew he had no chance of winning today's Motion. I suppose that's why he sent you to the

slaughter. Please thank Dwayne on my behalf for the gift of the easy five grand. Good day, Ms. Fawcett. Have a safe trip back to Wichita."

CHAPTER 16 (Motion Aftermath)

I drove back to Pittsburg and deposited the check into my trust account.

I phoned Joan's friend from my office and left a message for Joan and Harold to contact me.

Later in the afternoon they walked in to find out why I needed to talk with them.

"I was successful this morning at the court house in Girard. The insurance company tried to have our lawsuit dismissed. They lost the Motion and we were awarded $5,000 in costs. My thirty percent share of that award is $1,500 and you're entitled to the remaining $3,500. I need you to open a bank account today so that you can deposit this check into it. I'd suggest that you open your account at my credit union so there won't be any delay in you accessing the money."

"This is wonderful," Joan gushed. "We were so lucky to have seen your advertisement in the newspaper."

"What comes next?" Harold inquired.

"It's very possible that nothing will happen for quite a while. The usual next stage is discoveries in which each side attempts to obtain information about the strength of their opponent's case. I'll keep you posted. It would also be helpful if you installed a land line telephone at your home so that I can contact you more quickly."

"We'll do that today and let you know our new phone number," Joan replied.

After they left I sent an email to Dwayne Rackham at CALCYMON LLP, his law firm. In the message I demanded production of all insurance company correspondence, email and phone records relating to my clients' insurance claim against his client.

The purpose of my request was to determine which employees at CONEQUITAL INSURANCE I needed to examine under oath prior to the trial.

Joan and Harold had called their adjuster a few times early on following Harold's accident but had their phone disconnected for non-payment and thereafter said that they had sent regular letters asking about the status of the claim and in those letters provided updates about their desperate financial situation. They hadn't kept a copy of those letters.

Establishing outright negligence or even malice on the part of CONEQUITAL would go a long way in persuading a Judge to award substantial damages.

Now about all I could do was wait for a reply. If no response was forthcoming in the next couple of weeks, then I'd have to issue subpoenas for production of the documents.

In order to demonstrate that I was serious, in a separate email I requested an appointment in order to examine the adjuster who had signed the various letters to my clients. His name was Byron Cleave and I realized that I'd have to drive to Wichita to carry out that discovery.

I'd been fortunate to attract Harold and Joan as my first clients. Dealing with their file had kept me busy since they wandered into my office.

The fact that no other potential clients had yet surfaced indicated that it was difficult for a complete stranger to operate a law practice in a small town.

I certainly wasn't ready to take up some elderly activity like euchre or lawn bowling to fill more of my time.

CHAPTER 17 (A Blunt Advocate)

Late on Monday afternoon my telephone rang with a most interesting call.

"My name is Candace Blake and my friend's son has suddenly found himself in a bit of a legal bind. Last week he was served with some legal documents. I happened to recall seeing the announcement in the newspaper that you recently opened your law office."

"What sort of documents did he receive?"

"I'd have to show them to you and explain the background. It's too complicated to explain over the telephone."

"I'm reluctant to agree to that without knowing even what area of the law is involved. I'm a sole practitioner and plan on restricting my practice to litigation."

"You're my friend's last hope. None of the other attorneys in town will assist her son for fear of upsetting Johnathan Baxter. Have you heard of him?"

"Yes I have."

"Mr. Baxter through his attorney will crucify my friend's son. Surely your professional probity is attuned to preventing injustice."

"Why isn't your friend's son contacting me directly?"

"He's a member of a younger generation which has no spunk and is willing to get walked over by powerful and ruthless adversaries."

"Will the young man be accompanying you if I agree to listen to him?"

"I'm afraid not. He has gone to Wichita with his mother Jennifer Mackintosh for a medical appointment and won't return until Wednesday which will be too late. The legal documents indicate that the court will hear the matter tomorrow morning in Girard."

"This has all the earmarks of a hopeless mess but I will look over the documents and listen to your version of the facts. I need to be crystal clear that I'm not yet agreeing to represent the young man. Can you live with that condition?"

"I'll be over in ten minutes. Thank you for your kindness."

I couldn't be bothered to change into a suit. The yellow sweatshirt which had become my standard office attire was comfortable. This appointment sounded like a farce anyway.

It was less than ten minutes when a very attractive raven-haired woman entered the room, looked at me, then at the onslaught of purple and burst out laughing.

"My decorator assured me that purple was a happy color. I guess he was correct. It has certainly made you smile. I'm Donald Saunders. I assume that you're Candace Blake."

"Forgive my reaction but the phrase that stuck in my mind when I saw you dressed like a jogger sitting in this designer's nightmare was 'ABANDON HOPE ALL WHO ENTER HERE.' Please forgive my rude but involuntary reaction."

"We attorneys of necessity have very thick skin. Since my office has delighted you so thoroughly, would you like a quick tour of the rest of my home before we get down to business?"

"Yes, I'll risk it despite the fact that I left my heart pills at home."

"Please, young lady. Follow me."

Already I was enjoying the banter. The lady looked to be in her late forties and was clearly well-educated despite her blunt approach to life.

I swung open the French doors and Candace gasped as she was inundated with bright green.

We walked into the living-room where she couldn't restrain a sarcastic remark.

"This room is absolutely hideous. Are you demented?"

"It's my clients who must be demented to entrust their legal problems into my care. Have you seen enough or shall we complete the deluxe tour?"

"Let's chance it. I've certainly learned one thing about you. It's glaringly apparent that you've never been married."

"Perhaps my wife has a thing for color."

"Cloud white is a color. These rooms scream out that the owner was on a bad drug trip when he ventured into the paint store."

Candace followed me upstairs. The stairs and upstairs hallway sported bright pink carpet and walls.

She was rendered speechless for a long moment and her jaw had gaped open.

Finally she commented.

"You've outdone yourself, Donald. This explosion of color is even more outrageous than the main floor. What on earth were you thinking?"

"In my defence, I must inform you that the rainbow décor was already in place when I purchased the home last month on the day before Christmas. It just happens that I love the color scheme. This concludes today's tour. Let's adjourn to the purple room and evaluate your young friend's problem."

"Will your advice be as off-putting as your home?"

"That's a distinct possibility."

Candace handed me the documents which had been served on her friend's son.

CHAPTER 18 (A Dog's Breakfast)

I perused the legal papers.

"Johnathan Baxter's attorney has thrown everything but the kitchen sink into this application. Give me the concise English version of the situation."

"Brady Mackintosh was the boyfriend of Amy Baxter until about a month ago when they had a big argument and broke up. They resided together in a home owned by one of Johnathan Baxter's companies and they both worked for one of Johnathan's businesses. Amy is Johnathan's granddaughter."

"Where do Brady and Amy live now?"

"Amy moved out temporarily until Brady leaves the house."

"Why is he still living there?"

"Brady got angry and is just being stubborn. Johnathan fired Brady the day after Amy moved out of the home and now Brady is taking the position that he can't be evicted while the rent moratorium is in place. That's apparently the main purpose of the application."

"Did Brady actually pay the rent?"

"In fact Johnathan wasn't charging any rent."

"I guess that explains why Johnathan is seeking an order declaring Brady to be a house guest who refused to leave despite being told to go in writing. How long did Brady and Amy cohabit?"

"Amy already lived there when they started dating. Brady moved in last August."

"Do they have children?"

"No they don't. Brady is only twenty-two and Amy is perhaps a year older."

"What is it that Brady wants? Can't he just pack up his belongings and move in with his mother?"

"Brady realizes that he'll never find another job in Pittsburg. Nobody around here would dare antagonize Johnathan by hiring Brady. Brady doesn't have a cent to his name and Brady doesn't have a clue what he wants. My friend and her ex-husband spoiled Brady rotten and as a result, he's incapable of thinking for himself. He has no money to pay anything back to Johnathan."

"What do you expect me to do for him?"

"Johnathan has already repossessed the car his company was permitting Brady to use. I don't expect miracles but if the Judge makes a ruling in favor of Johnathan, then Brady will have that debt hanging over his head for years. Johnathan will do everything in his power to make Brady's life miserable. He'll seize his bank account if Brady ever saves any money and Johnathan will garnishee any wages if Brady manages to find a job in some other city."

"The employer is seeking reimbursement for what they deem the personal portion of Brady's use for both the vehicle and the smart phone. What do you know about that issue?"

"Brady said that paying a portion of the vehicle and smart phone costs for his personal use was never even mentioned while he worked for the company but he doesn't have anything in writing disputing that claim."

"It's highly unusual for an attorney to represent a client without actually being hired by that client. Are you suggesting that my goal would be to persuade the Judge not to award any compensation or costs in the matter?"

"That's the best Brady could hope for. I'll pay your legal account if you take on the case."

"I applaud your generosity but I need to speak with Brady personally. Can you reach him by telephone right now?"

"I can text my friend on her smart phone and have her call you here."

"Please do so. While we're waiting for the return call, I'll try to extract more information from you about Brady's situation. Do you have any papers other than the notice of application?"

"Jennifer gave me Brady's entire file before they left for Wichita. I glanced at the materials but didn't notice anything relevant."

Candace handed me the file.

I picked through the papers while we waited for Brady or his mother to phone.

Thirty minutes passed and it was now five o'clock. I was still poring through the messy file.

"I'm so sorry, Mr. Saunders. Jennifer must have her smart phone turned off. Brady no longer has such a device. His smart phone was owned by the company and was confiscated along with the vehicle he drove. Will you try to help Brady anyway?"

"I'll drive to Girard tomorrow morning and appear at the hearing. If I'm unsuccessful in persuading the Judge not to award a monetary settlement including court costs then I won't charge any fee. Certainly even having a color-challenged lawyer on the case can't be any worse than having absolutely no representation."

"Can I come with you?"

"I suppose it can't hurt. It's possible that I'll have a few questions which you may be able to answer after I've looked over Brady's entire file."

We arranged that Candace would arrive here at eight-fifteen, leave her car in my driveway and that we would drive to Girard in my vehicle.

CHAPTER 19 (Vivacious Company)

Candace departed and I made myself some supper before tackling Brady's thick mess of a file.

The file contained a bit of everything including various photos. At least it allowed me to know what Brady, Amy and Johnathan Baxter looked like.

Brady wasn't a complete dummy. He had kept hard copies of various emails he received from Amy as well as copies of his pay stubs.

Two emails in particular caught my attention regarding Brady's occupation of the home. One was dated last July from the corporation which owned the property and it casually used the term "tenancy" in an email to Brady and Amy which also stated that no rent would be payable without thirty days' written notice first being given.

A more intriguing email to Brady came directly from Amy. It was dated the 1st day of August, 2020 and stated that Brady would be entitled to four months of severance if his employment was terminated prior to April of 2021 and that he would have the use of a company car and smart phone. No mention was made one way or the other regarding personal use of those perks.

It appeared that Brady moved into the home with Amy the following weekend.

The rent email was extremely valuable to Brady's case because it didn't appear that any notice of a rent increase had in fact been given. Baxter's corporation had simply demanded that Brady move out immediately and incorrectly advised him that he was a non-paying house guest only and had no legal right to remain in the home.

The job severance email was more problematic. It was very unlikely that Amy had the legal authority to bind the numbered company which employed her.

When I set up this law office, I subscribed to various legal websites, one of which permitted me for a small fee to check corporate records on-line.

I called up the company information on the corporation which owned the house and determined that Johnathan Baxter was the sole shareholder and corporate officer.

The numbered company which employed Brady and Amy was much more interesting.

Johnathan Baxter was also the sole shareholder but there were two corporate officers. Baxter was president and treasurer but Amy Baxter was the secretary.

I perused the incorporation documents and determined that agreements only needed the consent of one officer, not both. Checks had to be signed by both officers only if the amount was higher than $1,000.

I downloaded the relevant corporate records and printed off a hard copy.

Nothing else in Brady's file seemed relevant but it wasted two additional hours of my time before I reached that conclusion.

On Tuesday morning I dressed in a dark grey pinstripe suit and took a bit of time with my hair to make it appear professionally styled. I brought along my legal robes even though it was unlikely that I'd have to gown up in order to appear on the application.

Candace arrived a few minutes early.

"You certainly clean up beautifully, Mr. Saunders. Today might not be as hopeless as I'd feared."

We left Pittsburg precisely at eight-fifteen.

"How long have you been an attorney?" Candace inquired.

"I joined the Kansas state legal bar exactly one year ago but I only set up my law practice on January 4th of this year. In fact Brady is only my second client."

"What did you do before becoming an attorney?"

"My past will remain a mystery, Candace. I arrived in Kansas a month ago on December 21st and closed my colorful house purchase on Christmas Eve morning. Running my tiny business is my retirement hobby. That's enough about me. Tell me a bit about yourself."

"I grew up here in Pittsburg but attended university and graduate school in Massachusetts. I spent my career in Boston and New York City employed by various computer software companies. When the pandemic shut most businesses down last March, I accepted a buyout of my contract and moved back here. My father died several years ago but my mother still resides in Pittsburg. Do you have family?"

"No I don't. I was married when I was much younger but have been divorced for more than twenty-five years. Fortunately we had no children."

"How old are you?"

"I'm sixty-six. How old are you?"

"It's impertinent to ask a woman that question. Perhaps that insensitivity explains why you're divorced."

I knew that Candace was teasing.

"If I didn't know how to successfully pry, I wouldn't be the country's most color-coordinated lawyer."

"You look older than your chronological age. You're obviously addicted to color. You should dye your hair."

"Which room would you suggest that my hair match? I thought you were a fan of cloud white. That's why I didn't dye my hair purple this morning. I was only trying to please you."

"At least you've got a decent sense of humor for an attorney. By the way, I'm sixty-two."

"I'm stunned. I didn't peg you as a day over sixty-one and a half."

"Oh you mean bastard," Candace exclaimed as she punched me on the shoulder.

The banter ceased as we pulled into the parking lot near the county court house.

"On a more serious note, Donald, are we going to get creamed in court this morning?"

"Oh ye of little faith," I replied with a smile.

CHAPTER 20 (Angry Rich Guy)

We stopped at the court office where I inquired whether it was necessary to robe up to appear on the Baxter versus Mackintosh application. It was not.

Candace and I made our way to the small courtroom where the matter was to be heard. Again Judge Jane Plowright was presiding.

We were the first ones to enter the courtroom although the lights were all turned on.

"It might be prudent for you to sit somewhere near the back on the opposite side to where I'll be sitting. Given the animosity involved with this proceeding, it's best if we don't provide any evidence that you're with me. I'll meet you at my vehicle after the hearing concludes. We shouldn't walk out together."

I sat down and arranged my documents in such a way that I could access anything easily.

A few minutes before ten o'clock, Desmond Carlyle arrived with an older man I recognized as Johnathan Baxter. Amy Baxter was also present.

I nodded hello to Carlyle who glared at me without responding.

Judge Plowright entered the courtroom from a door near her bench and we all rose.

"Good morning, everyone; please introduce yourselves."

Carlyle announced that he was the attorney for the applicants.

"I'm Donald Saunders representing the respondent, Brady Mackintosh. I have to admit that I haven't actually spoken with Mr. Mackintosh or his mother. A friend of the family contacted me yesterday and begged me to attend today to protect the young man's interests. I'm fully prepared to do so but in the circumstances, I'm also willing to consent to an adjournment if the court so orders."

Carlyle stood up and objected to any adjournment.

The Judge agreed with him.

"Let's get started, gentlemen. This proceeding needs to be completed by noon. Don't disappoint me."

Carlyle explained the reason for the application and set out the facts.

Then he briefly laid out each of the two main issues for which his clients were seeking redress.

"Beginning with the most crucial matter, Judge, which is an order compelling Brady Mackintosh to vacate the property owned by Baxter Properties Limited, I submit the three separate letters demanding vacant possession. I would point out that the respondent continues to reside in the home. As to the second issue, namely reimbursement for personal use of the car and smart phone as well as a return of a portion of the respondent's wages, we have utilized a work time versus non-work time evaluation."

Judge Plowright interrupted.

"It will be less confusing if we deal fully with each issue individually, starting with the occupation of the property. What is your response to that issue, Mr. Saunders?"

"Our position is that Brady Mackintosh was at all times a tenant of the home even though no rental was being charged."

"That's absurd," Carlyle thundered.

"Perhaps my learned colleague has failed to examine the correspondence regarding the issue. I submit a hard copy of an email addressed to Brady and Amy from the corporate owner of the property which clearly describes the occupation as a tenancy and also indicates that no rent will be payable unless thirty days' written notice is first given. To the best of our knowledge, no such notice has yet been delivered which means that Brady Mackintosh is indeed a tenant, the current rent remains at zero and in fact he can likely take advantage of the rent moratorium and remain in possession."

"I strenuously object, Judge. We haven't received a copy of that alleged email."

"Before Mr. Carlyle has a coronary, Judge Plowright, I should assuage his concern by stating that my client is willing to vacate the premises on or before Saturday, January 23rd, as long as the other monetary issues regarding this application are dealt with satisfactorily."

"Is that acceptable to you, Mr. Carlyle?"

"Yes it is, Judge. Thank you."

"Let's move on to the compensation issue. Enlighten us, Mr. Carlyle."

"We've calculated the personal use percentage of the company vehicle and smart phone as being half of the total cost of those items. The applicants want an order against the respondent in the total amount of $1,100. We've been generous in the circumstances and did not include any loss of interest or depreciation on the vehicle. Only the gas, repairs and licence costs have been listed."

"Do you object to that method of calculation, Mr. Saunders?"

"It's a small enough amount that I can live with my esteemed colleague's figures. My client claims that he was never informed that he would have to pay any personal use portion of the cost of the vehicle or smart phone. Does Mr. Carlyle have anything in writing regarding such a provision?"

"We don't, Judge. It was purely a verbal agreement."

"Does that concern you, Mr. Saunders?"

"Since the amounts seem reasonable, I won't dispute the applicant's allegation that there actually was an agreement. The much more contentious issue relates to the applicant's claim for a return of a portion of Mr. Mackintosh's wages."

"I understand, Mr. Saunders. Mr. Carlyle, the ball is in your court. Please explain why your clients are demanding a refund of $1,200 of the respondent's wages."

"Mr. Mackintosh was paid $4,000 per month. He began employment on August 4th, 2020 and was terminated on December 28th of that same year. The employer had paid an advance Christmas bonus of $1,200 to Mackintosh on December 24th but that was conditional on the young man remaining with the company until he had completed his first full year of employment."

"What is your response, Mr. Saunders?"

"As with the personal use of the vehicle and smart phone matters, am I to assume that nothing was reduced to writing regarding the Christmas bonus potential repayment?"

Carlyle replied that the condition was conveyed verbally to Mr. Mackintosh.

"Do you have further comments, Mr. Saunders?"

"If my arithmetic skills are still accurate, I've calculated that the applicants want a total of $2,300 back from my client and also want him to vacate the home. We are willing to accommodate those somewhat suspect demands if the applicant pays Mr. Mackintosh the sum of $16,000 representing the severance pay the employer had agreed in writing would be due to my client if his position was terminated prior to April of 2021. I submit herewith a copy of the email from the employer clearly setting out that severance term."

Carlyle leapt up from his chair and made it to the Judge's bench by the time I was handing the email up to her.

Judge Plowright looked at the email and then let Carlyle have a look.

"Mr. Saunders appears to be correct in his assertion, Mr. Carlyle. What is your response?"

"Please let me consult with my client for moment and show him this document."

Carlyle handed the email to Johnathan who read it and then showed it to Amy. They whispered among themselves for a moment.

"This email is invalid, Judge. It was sent by Amy Baxter, not by the employer. Also, there is no consideration mentioned which means that legally it can't be considered to be a valid agreement."

"Do you wish to counter that argument, Mr. Saunders?"

"I do, Your Honor. To begin, let me express my disgust that the applicants are willing to claim that alleged verbal agreements are fully binding but reject this agreement which was actually reduced to writing. The consideration was Mr. Mackintosh accepting the job which was being offered to him."

I walked back to my table and grabbed the corporate records search results which I handed to the Judge.

"These are the corporate search records for the numbered company which was the employer of Mr. Mackintosh. As you will note therein, Amy Baxter is the secretary of the corporation and has the authority to make agreements. The company is bound by her email promising my client a severance payment equal to four months of his salary."

"Mr. Saunders seems to be correct on this point. How do you respond, Mr. Carlyle?"

"Again, please give me a moment to consult with my clients."

Johnathan Baxter was clearly livid with his attorney. Amy was frozen in place like a statue. A heated exchange took place but I was unable to decipher the words because they were whispering vigorously at each other.

Carlyle returned to the front of the courtroom.

"We dispute Mr. Saunders' interpretation of that email."

"I see. Do either of you gentlemen have other legal points to make or is it time for me to rule on these issues?"

Carlyle spoke first.

"We respectfully request that the court rule in the applicants' favor on each issue put forward and that respondent be made to pay our legal costs. Thank you, Judge."

"What is your position, Mr. Saunders?"

"Although I'm content with having this court rule on each individual claim put forward by the applicants, my client is still willing to acquiesce to every individual point of contention as long as the court orders the applicant employer to pay the sum of $16,000 less the $2,300 needed to fulfil the other monetary claims. If Mr. Carlyle is willing to consent to such an order and also to waive his claim for costs, then I will also consent and waive our own claim for costs."

Carlyle was obviously uncomfortable. He asked for a moment to discuss the matter with his clients.

After several minutes Carlyle advised that his clients were agreeable to such a consent order.

I indicated that I too was satisfied subject only to the Judge ensuring that the $13,700 be paid immediately to myself in trust with my undertaking not to disburse the funds to my client until he had fully vacated the home which he would do on or before Saturday, January 23rd.

The Judge made the consent order and Carlyle wrote out his own trust check payable to me and handed it to me.

We both thanked the Judge and she left the courtroom.

I noticed Candace slipping out the main courtroom door.

Johnathan Baxter approached me.

"You've just put yourself on my permanent naughty list, Saunders. Interfering in my mortgage foreclosure was bad enough but rubbing my nose in my own excrement today was the last straw."

"It's a shame that we've gotten off on the wrong foot, sir. Our paths are certain to cross over and over again. Apparently I'm the only attorney in town who isn't afraid to stand up to you. Open acrimony between us will make future settlements quite difficult. Both of us would benefit by maintaining a collegial relationship."

"That won't happen, Saunders. You'll soon find out how virulent an enemy I can be."

"That's short-sighted of you, sir. Cooperation between us would be best for everybody."

"I can afford to be short-sighted. Can you?"

I smiled.

"I'm sorry, Baxter but with that attitude there's only one piece of advice I can give you."

"And what might that be?"

"You'll need to construct a pipeline directly from your wallet to my pocket."

"Fuck you, shyster," Baxter snarled as he spun around and marched out of the courtroom with Amy Baxter and

Desmond Carlyle shuffling behind him like two harshly disciplined puppy dogs.

CHAPTER 21 (Wrapping Up the File)

Candace was waiting at my car.

"I can't believe what happened in there, Donald. You were magnificent."

"I only did it to impress you. It's fortunate that you didn't wait around for me."

"Why is that?"

"Baxter tore a strip off me and vowed to make my life miserable. I tried to be polite but then got a bit flippant with him. Let's just downplay the confrontation and say I won't be on his cocktail party invite list anytime soon."

"He really is a powerful man around this county. It's such a shame that you've antagonized him all because you did a favor for a spoiled brat."

"Speaking of Brady Mackintosh, has he or his mother contacted you yet?"

"No they haven't. I sent text messages last evening and again early this morning but they haven't responded. They're due back tomorrow around noon."

"It's imperative that Brady vacate the home immediately and provide me with his keys. As soon as he has done that, then I'll deliver the keys to Desmond Carlyle and have him contact

Baxter to confirm that Brady and his belongings are out of the house."

"I promised to pay your legal account and I'll honor that commitment."

"That won't be necessary. I'll pay my account from the settlement funds. I've expended at least five hours on the file so my fee will be $1,000 plus a few bucks for disbursements. You and I achieved an excellent result for Brady. I hope he appreciates what you did for him by persevering until you found an attorney who would represent the kid. The Judge would likely have found totally in Baxter's favor if no one on Brady's behalf had bothered to show up."

"I hear you. Brady will now have a bit of money to get established in another town. I'll have to reward you by treating you to dinner in the near future."

"That's an excellent idea."

A few minutes later we pulled into my office driveway.

Candace promised to corral Brady tomorrow and coerce him to get himself and his belongings out of Amy's house.

We tentatively arranged our dinner date for Friday.

There were no messages on my answering machine when I went into my office.

I walked to my credit union and deposited Carlyle's check into my trust account.

Then I prepared my legal account which I wouldn't pay until Brady had fulfilled his end of the bargain.

On Wednesday afternoon Candace called. She and her friend were driving Brady to the house to remove his stuff. They would drop in to my office in about an hour to hand over the keys.

When they arrived, Brady reinforced my opinion that kids were more trouble than joy. He was totally unimpressed with the result of the court hearing and had the gall to moan about my legal account.

Both Candace and Jennifer tore a strip off Brady and reminded him that by not bothering to show up in person or with counsel, he would have been crucified by Johnathan Baxter.

I had Brady sign a simple Retainer Agreement, an acknowledgement that he had fully vacated the property as well as an authorization for me to pay my legal account in full from the settlement money.

Candace had her own vehicle and she volunteered to deliver the acknowledgement and the house keys to Desmond Carlyle's office. That prevented any possible unpleasantness between Baxter's lawyer and me.

I also phoned Carlyle to say that Brady had vacated the home and that the keys were being delivered in the next few minutes.

Desmond was polite and said that he would have Amy check the house immediately and report back to him at which point he would shoot me an email confirming that Brady had vacated and that I could release the settlement proceeds.

Later that afternoon I received the email.

I walked to the credit union, deposited my legal fee into my firm account and wrote my trust check payable to Brady Mackintosh for the remaining $12,652.

It struck me that if Brady had consulted me personally, I would have insisted on a contingency fee of thirty percent of any award.

The little shit had saved himself more than three grand by being totally irresponsible.

Jennifer drove Brady to my office to pick up the check within ten minutes of my call that it was ready. I had banged off a brief report letter explaining how the settlement amount had been calculated and handed it to Brady along with the check. The report letter would protect my own ass if Brady changed his

mind at some point in the near future and decided to sue me for negligence.

CHAPTER 22 (First Date)

Candace arrived to pick me up for our dinner date on Friday evening at six-thirty.

We had agreed to dress casually. Candace had suggested a local diner called Jim's Steak House. She drove.

Once we were seated and had placed our drink orders, I asked Candace how she was enjoying residing back in her home town.

"I only returned because Mom was struggling. She still lived in her own home but the pandemic shutdowns curtailed all of her former social activities. I moved in with her last May even though Pittsburg, Kansas is not my idea of a retirement paradise. Tell me again why you decided to move here."

"I had planned on keeping my past secret but I guess I can trust you with the truth. I was senior partner in a law firm in Buffalo, New York. My partners voted me out of the firm on December 17th."

"Why did they do that?"

"They were significantly younger than me and they wanted to expand our offices and take on the legal work for an insurance company which I knew to be extraordinarily ruthless. At first I was shocked at being kicked out of my own law firm. The terms of our partnership agreement prevented me from competing anywhere in New York State for a period of five years. It seemed that my attorney days were over."

"And yet here you are. How did that happen?"

"Last January I was recruited to assist in a complex real estate lawsuit here in Kansas. The firm who needed my help pulled some strings and got me accepted as a member of the Kansas legal bar. That case settled and I never needed to travel to Kansas but suddenly I had a choice other than full retirement. I decided to be a small town attorney and chose Pittsburg mostly for its attractive size and moderately appealing climate."

"If you were a successful lawyer in Buffalo, why did you purchase that rainbow monstrosity instead of finding a more upscale location?"

"The house of many colors was available immediately and the price was so attractive that I felt that even if I disliked Pittsburg, I could resell the home and move to another city. There weren't many apartments available because of the local university and the two which were for rent were overpriced. The carrying costs of the house are much cheaper than renting a place. Also, the house is large enough that I can use the dining-room as my home occupation legal office."

"How much did you pay for it?"

"I paid $45,000 and looked after my own closing costs."

"That didn't fully answer my question. Why didn't you buy an upscale home?"

"I saw no reason to do so. In Buffalo I had a lovely condominium but got tired of commuting to the office so I sold the unit a year ago and rented a small furnished condo within easy walking distance of my office. I'm a bit embarrassed to admit that my law practice was my life. The hours I worked in Buffalo were quite brutal. Also, I'm a bit on the frugal side of the ledger."

"You had mentioned that you were married once but divorced more than twenty-five years ago. Did you not have a lady friend in Buffalo?"

"I very occasionally had a date but never put much of a priority on finding a life partner. I guess my law office was my companion."

"That's rather sad."

"I hear you. I'm already much happier living in Pittsburg and running my new law office as a hobby rather than a career. That's enough about me for now. Tell me more about yourself. Have you never been married?"

"No I haven't although I've had two live-in relationships. The first one lasted for twelve years in Boston. When Jack and I realized that the thrill was gone from our romance, we sold our home. I accepted a job in New York City and several years later met a fellow named Craig who worked on Wall Street. We cohabited for four years and in fact just broke up on Christmas Eve in 2019. I moved here five months later. This is the closest thing to a date I've had in Pittsburg."

"Are you happy with your retirement?"

"That's too positive a description but I'm okay with not working. I'm very comfortable financially and feel that I've been a Godsend for Mom."

"How have you been filling your time?"

"I write the occasional article about computer issues and I've even started a mystery novel. Because of the Covid-19 restrictions, it hasn't been possible to carve out any social life."

The server appeared at our table and we placed our food orders.

The topic then shifted over to Johnathan Baxter.

"I'm so sorry that my desperate plea to you to assist Brady with his problem has wound up offending Johnathan Baxter."

"It was inevitable since I seem to be the only attorney in town willing to stand up to him."

"Baxter is beyond ruthless. He'll find a way to make your life miserable."

"My other legal file also involved Mr. Baxter. He and Desmond Carlyle already disliked me before I showed up in the courtroom on Tuesday."

"What was that matter about?"

"Baxter was in the process of foreclosing on an older couple. They wandered in my office just like you did at the last possible minute. I managed to get Baxter off their back but their legal matter is still very much active. It relates to an insurance claim and will likely take many months or even longer to resolve. Some insurance companies are wicked when it comes to paying legitimate claims."

The rest of the evening passed quickly and very pleasantly. Candace was very easy to talk to.

She drove me home at ten o'clock when the restaurant closed up. Since this evening was her way of repaying me for helping Brady Mackintosh, I merely thanked Candace for a lovely evening

and said that I hoped we could share a meal again sometime.

CHAPTER 23 (Rapid Treachery)

On Wednesday the 27th of January I learned the bitter lesson that no good deed goes unpunished.

Two nasty and upsetting things occurred.

The first surprise was a morning email from an attorney in town named Claudia Norman stating that she had been consulted by Brady Mackintosh and was shocked to learn from him that I had attended at a court hearing on his behalf without his prior knowledge or consent.

The attorney put me on notice that she had sent an ethics complaint on Brady's behalf to the Kansas Bar Association and to the Kansas Office of the Disciplinary Administrator.

I was damn angry but managed to calm myself before phoning the lawyer.

The bitch refused to take my call.

That meant that I'd have to wait until I received a phone call or correspondence from the disciplinary office before I could tell my side of the story.

It was pointless responding to Ms. Norman. The complaint was now out of her hands.

It was ironic. In my many years of legal practice in Buffalo, I had never been subject to a complaint to the New York State Bar Association.

Already it had happened in Kansas and I'd only had two clients.

Early in the afternoon the other shoe dropped.

I was served with a Statement of Claim from the office of Desmond Carlyle on behalf of Johnathan Baxter's two companies which were involved with the Mackintosh matter.

In the writ they claimed a return of the $13,700 Baxter's corporations had paid to me plus their legal costs of the January 19th hearing.

This was really just a nuisance claim but wouldn't help my reputation in town.

I phoned Candace who was surprisingly evasive.

"Can't you tell me anything about why Brady has decided to turn on me?"

"Jennifer and I are no longer speaking. Apparently Brady and Amy reconciled on the weekend. I'm so sorry to abandon you, Donald. Johnathan Baxter has some leverage over my mother and I can't let him ruin her life over the likes of Brady Mackintosh. Please don't call me again."

I was dumbfounded when the call ended.

Small towns were just as corrupt as big cities.

I pondered whether Candace had in fact set me up right from the beginning but discarded that notion. No one, not even a skilled actress could have pulled off such a deception. I was curious about what leverage Baxter had on a little old lady but couldn't even hazard a guess.

Any fantasy I might have had about forming a romance with Candace had been flushed right down the toilet.

I spent the rest of the afternoon crafting my Statement of Defence relating to Baxter's Small Claims Court action.

Judge Plowright had seemed totally unbiased but the possibility of Baxter having a Small Claims Court Judge in his pocket was a real concern.

Johnathan was showing me how vengeful he was and also how much influence he wielded in this county.

On Thursday morning I drove to Girard and filed my Statement of Defence with the Small Claims Court Clerk.

I had toyed with the idea of counterclaiming for damages but wisely decided not to weaken my defence. The facts alone should be sufficient to have the case thrown out.

Carlyle had been crafty in keeping the claim under the Small Claims Court limit. If he had asked for higher damages, then it would have to be dealt with in the higher court where costs were awarded to winning parties.

Although both Carlyle and I had asked for costs, it was highly unusual for them to be awarded. Small Claims Court was supposed to be more congenial and less adversarial.

CHAPTER 24 (Complaint Settled)

The Kansas Bar Association was very proactive in dealing with Brady Mackintosh's ethics complaint against me.

On Friday morning I received a phone call from a claims administrator.

After introducing herself as Penelope Crawford and confirming that I had received a copy of the complaint from Brady Mackintosh's attorney, the administrator asked me to explain my side of the issue.

"I was contacted by a woman named Candace Blake who was a close friend of Brady's mother Jennifer Mackintosh. Brady had been served with legal documents the week before and his court hearing was being heard the following morning in the county seat of Girard."

"Had you dealt with Brady, his mother or her friend previously?"

"No. They were all strangers."

I explained what the court matter was about and how Candace texted Brady's mother at my request so that I could speak with Brady directly because he and Jennifer were in Wichita and wouldn't be returning to Pittsburg until the day after the court hearing.

"Why didn't you refuse to handle the matter when you were unable to obtain instructions from Brady?"

"Candace moaned that she had tried to locate a lawyer on Brady's behalf but none of the local attorneys would represent him because his opponent in court was Johnathan Baxter who was a powerful businessman. It was apparent to Candace, and I agreed with her, that if no one showed up on Brady's behalf, then the Judge would find in Baxter's favor and award costs against Brady."

"What happened at the court hearing?"

I related the gist of the individual claims by Baxter and the settlement that was concluded in the courtroom.

"It appears that you obtained an excellent result at the hearing, Mr. Saunders."

"Brady and Jennifer were thrilled with the result the following afternoon when they returned to Pittsburg and met with me. Brady vacated the home that day and I paid him the funds the following day after Baxter confirmed that Brady was gone from the property and had left it undamaged."

"Why have they changed their mind?"

"I assume that Johnathan Baxter has put pressure on them to do so. Brady and Amy have reconciled and he's again residing with her in the same home he had vacated the previous week. Baxter and I had words after the court hearing and he vowed to make my life miserable. In fact his companies are now suing me in Small Claims Court for the $13,700 they paid Brady Mackintosh."

"That's outrageous."

"It's even more sinister than that. Candace won't speak to me about these recent developments because Baxter has some leverage over Candace's mother. I guess I poked my nose under the wrong bush when I took on Johnathan Baxter by defending Brady's legal rights to have his side of the argument properly explained to the Judge."

"Is there anything you can send me that will enable our office to respond to Brady Mackintosh's complaint against you?"

"I can email you a copy of the Retainer Agreement I had Brady sign the day following the hearing as well as a copy of my report letter and legal account."

"How much did you charge Mr. Mackintosh for your legal representation?"

"I only charged him $1,000 plus $28 for the disbursements which were the corporate records searches I had performed. In fact I had spent significantly more than five hours on Brady's file. He had given Candace his entire file and I pored over it all evening. Doing so enabled me to discover reasonable legal defences against each of Baxter's claims. In addition to the time spent examining the file, I of course also drove to Girard and back in order to attend the court hearing."

At Ms. Crawford's request, I emailed the documents to her while we continued to converse on the phone. She confirmed that she had received them and then perused them while asking me a couple of pertinent questions about why Candace Blake had Brady's file.

"I'm totally convinced, Mr. Saunders. Mr. Mackintosh's complaint is frivolous and entirely unjustified. I'll respond immediately to Claudia Norman's letter and forward a copy to you. May I ask why you didn't contact Ms. Norman directly?"

"I phoned her office as soon as I had calmed down after first reading her email but she refused to take my call."

"I'm shocked that anyone would complain about their attorney in these circumstances. For crying out loud, you even attempted to seek an adjournment but the plaintiffs objected and the Judge ordered that the hearing proceed. You acted perfectly."

"Thank you, Penelope for being so reasonable and listening to my side of the story."

I felt a lot better after the call ended. At least that aspect of the mess appeared to be over.

CHAPTER 25 (More Treachery)

Saturday morning brought more distressing news.

Harold and Joan Els knocked on my office door. I was cleaning up my breakfast dishes and let them in.

"We need to speak with you," Harold mumbled.

"Sure, folks; please have a seat but I haven't got anything to report on your insurance claim. I'm still waiting for the company to send me some documentation I've requested."

"We parked on another street and walked here so that nobody would know that we've come to see you," Joan began.

"Is there a problem of some kind?"

"A gentleman came to see us at home last evening. He said that he could get Dexter released on early parole next week but only if we met certain conditions."

In the back of my mind I sensed that Johnathan Baxter was up to no good again. I sighed involuntarily.

Joan continued.

"The first condition was that we lay out exactly what you had done on our behalf to get the foreclosure cancelled and our tax arrears paid."

“I understand. What did you tell the fellow?”

Harold replied.

“We told him the whole truth about coming to see you in an absolute panic on January 7th and telling you all about the terrible mess we were in. We also said how you sprung right into action and used your own money to pay off our mortgage and tax arrears as well as our insurance premium and utility arrears in addition to providing us with a bit of cash for food.”

“That’s fine, Harold. Don’t feel guilty about telling the truth.”

“After we told him about the day we met you and what you had done for us, the man phoned someone. Then he began asking us questions about our insurance claim. We showed him the Statement of Claim you had issued on our behalf and the letters you sent us which divvied up the money you squeezed out of the insurance company after the court hearing.”

“That’s interesting. What happened next?”

“The man made another phone call and then made us an offer we couldn’t refuse.”

“I’m listening.”

"If we make a complaint against you to the Kansas Bar Association, then all the money we owe you will be paid off which means that we'll own our home free and clear. Another lawyer will take over our insurance claim and we'll be guaranteed to receive at least the $135,000 to cover my loss of wages and we won't be charged any legal fee. We don't know what to do. You've been so good to us but our son's welfare is our biggest concern right now. The man said that if we didn't agree to the package deal, then he couldn't guarantee Dexter's safety in prison."

"I'm a sinking ship. Johnathan Baxter is out to prove that he was the wrong man to upset. It wasn't just your file. I had a court case against Johnathan and that caused additional acrimony. In fact he's already sued me over that other file. You don't have any choice. Take the deal and make the complaint. I won't charge any legal fee and I'll deal with the Kansas Bar Association."

Joan moaned, "But that would mean that we're turning on you when you were so kind and generous with us."

"In some ways you'll be doing me a favor. It's becoming clear to me that I can't operate a viable law practice in Pittsburg. With your insurance file off my desk, I can pack up my business and get on with my retirement. Don't feel bad about what's happening. I'm pleased that your financial situation and your son's life will improve drastically."

Harold and Joan thanked me for being so understanding and slunk away.

The writing was on the wall. I had crossed swords with the wrong guy. Fighting Johnathan Baxter was not the retirement hobby I wanted.

I would close up my legal practice as soon as the insurance file had been transferred to Harold and Joan's new attorney.

CHAPTER 26 (Complaint Number Two)

Baxter wasted no time.

On Sunday I was contacted by a law firm in Wichita. They advised that they had been retained by Harold and Joan Els to take over the insurance file from me and they emailed me the authorization which Harold and Joan had signed yesterday afternoon.

We agreed to a meeting here at my office on Monday morning at which time they would issue their check payable to me in the amount of $21,875 to cover all the money I had disbursed on behalf of my clients. In return I would sign an acknowledgement that I had transferred the file to their firm and had been paid in full for all my services on behalf of Mr. and Mrs. Els.

I prepared a detailed covering letter setting out the details of the money I had loaned my clients and indicated that upon payment of the total, I would sign the promissory note as being repaid in full.

The Monday meeting was very uneventful. The young attorney who arrived at my office clearly didn't have any knowledge of the clandestine arrangements between Baxter and my clients. In fact she complimented me on my success in defending Mr. and Mrs. Els against the insurance company's motion to dismiss the claim.

On Wednesday I received another phone call from Penelope Crawford with the Kansas Office of the Disciplinary Administrator.

"I'm afraid that I've got additional bad news," she began. "Our office has received another client complaint against you. I'll email you a copy of the complaint right now so that you can look it over and we can discuss the matter."

"I know when I'm beaten, Penelope. I've only had two clients so far and now I'm two for two in client complaints. Both files involved Johnathan Baxter."

"This latest complaint from Harold and Joan Els says that you loaned them substantial funds without first sending them for independent legal advice. That does seem to be a breach of the ethics rules."

I explained to Penelope the events which led me to advance $21,875 to pay off the mortgage balance, tax arrears and other outstanding bills and I emailed to her a copy of the promissory note showing that no interest was being charged.

"Again, no other law firm would deal with Mr. and Mrs. Els for fear of upsetting Johnathan Baxter. I'm quite wealthy. This rinky-dink legal office in Pittsburg was supposed to be merely my retirement hobby. My loan to the clients was fully paid off on Monday and my insurance claim file has been transferred to a law firm in Wichita."

"Where do you think they came up with the funds to pay you off?"

"Can my answer be kept confidential just between us?"

"That's highly unusual and I wouldn't feel comfortable agreeing to your request."

"I understand. In that case I'll be vague. A certain party who detests me has likely gifted the required money to my former clients and has also made promises regarding the insurance claim outcome itself and some unrelated matters. The goal is to embarrass me and in this instance, Mr. and Mrs. Els are the lucky recipients of extensive financial benefits if they cease using my legal services and make their complaint. I don't want that aspect of the situation to be investigated in any way."

"Why is that?"

"The person who loathes me has no scruples and I don't want him reneging on his promises to Harold and Joan."

"I see. That might be a problem. Once you submit your explanatory defence to the complaint, since the lack of independent legal advice regarding the client loan is a breach of professional conduct, our office will be forced to investigate unless your former clients are satisfied with your response and advise us accordingly."

"I can't see that happening. The instigator will demand that the complaint process continue. Is there any way to avoid that scenario?"

"The only reason that comes to mind would be if you cancelled your licence to practice law in Kansas. In that event, the complaint would be rendered moot and we would advise the complainants that you were no longer a Kansas attorney and that our jurisdiction to impose any penalty was thereby extinguished."

"I'm willing to do that. I have no intention of continuing my legal practice in Pittsburg or anywhere else in Kansas. What forms do you require from me?"

"Are you sure that's what you want to do? It seems totally unfair to you."

"I'm a pragmatist, Penelope. I'll sleep at night knowing that I was responsible for a tremendous benefit in the lives of Harold and Joan."

"You'll find the necessary forms on our website. I'd suggest that you submit your explanatory defence today and wait until tomorrow to send in the resignation forms."

I thanked Penelope for her understanding.

CHAPTER 27 (Closing Up Shop)

I carefully crafted my response to Harold and Joan's ethics complaint and emailed it to Penelope.

Then I attended at my credit union and closed out my trust and business accounts. The trust account had a zero balance and I transferred the money in my business account into my personal checking account at my old bank.

On Thursday I submitted the required forms to the Kansas Bar Association and to the state authority which dealt with lawyer licensing. I also sent a copy to Penelope Crawford.

The only tag end remaining was the nuisance Small Claims Court lawsuit filed by Desmond Carlyle on behalf of Johnathan Baxter's companies.

I decided to be humble in the hope of persuading Baxter to drop the matter since the lawsuit had no chance whatsoever of success.

I phoned Desmond Carlyle who actually took my call even though he was rude.

"What do you want, Saunders?"

"I wanted to inform you that I've turned in my Kansas law licence today. Baxter is too formidable an adversary and I know when I'm licked. I intend to move out of Pittsburg as soon as I've sold my home and I would like to settle our Small Claims Court lawsuit so that I don't have to return here in the future."

"I'll pass your surrender message on to my client."

Carlyle abruptly hung up on me.

Next I called Pete Conrad and he came to my home in order to give me an idea of what price my home might fetch in today's market.

Pete suggested that I ask $52,900 which would allow me to break even on the home after taking into consideration both my sale and purchase costs.

Pete also warned me that the décor would be my biggest impediment to finding a buyer.

I told Pete that I'd think about it for a few days. There was no point moving away until the Small Claims Court lawsuit was disposed of.

On Friday morning Carlyle phoned.

"My client is willing to give you two choices. You can pay us $10,000 and we'll drop the lawsuit or you can damn well wait for the case to come up for trial."

"Baxter isn't being reasonable. That does it. Your client asked for this. The lawsuit has absolutely no chance of success. I'll wait for the trial and

I'll subpoena Baxter as a witness whereupon I'll rub his sleazy nose in his own feces while I tear him to shreds on the witness stand. At the same time I'll make you look like a bumbling idiot for bringing the case in the first place. You're no match for me in a courtroom, Carlyle. But you probably already know that. Now I can't wait to meet you again in open court. I'll make sure to invite all the other local attorneys."

This time I hung up on Carlyle.

I was fuming.

My antagonistic response was unexpectedly successful.

Carlyle called back an hour later.

"Mr. Baxter has decided to give you a break, Saunders. I can meet you at the court office in Girard in an hour where we can execute a Mutual Release and the lawsuit will be withdrawn."

"I'm pleased to hear that. Waiting around Pittsburg for weeks or months wasn't my top choice now that I'm fully retired. I'll meet you at the court house in an hour."

I was greatly relieved at this fortuitous turn of events. Settling the lawsuit was the last legal impediment to a carefree retirement.

With any luck the house would sell quickly once I'd listed it and I could move out of this corrupt cesspool.

I drove to Girard and waited around for Carlyle to show up which he did precisely on time.

We signed the release forms and the lawsuit was withdrawn.

Carlyle and I were cordial to each other but nevertheless we made no small talk. It was strictly business between us.

I drove home and felt that another weight had been lifted off my shoulders.

CHAPTER 28 (Ultimate Treachery)

Most of the furniture in my house was of no use to me so I intended to include almost everything in the property sale. I was in a bit of a quandary concerning what to do with my antique desk and matching bookcase.

I was a bit of a neat freak and had kept the house relatively spotless which meant that there was little tidying up to do in preparation for house showings.

Before I actually listed the home for sale, it made sense to move my desk and bookcase up to one of the spare bedrooms along with the rest of my office equipment.

On Friday evening I drank some beer after cooking a fancier supper than usual.

Saturday was quiet.

I studied some maps and tried to determine where I'd like to live during the next phase of my life.

One possibility came to mind.

During my marriage Beth and I had taken several winter vacations to various southern locations, most of which were Caribbean cruises.

After we split up, I rarely travelled except at Christmas time. I had discovered that Las Vegas was an excellent destination for a gentleman travelling alone. There were no single supplements involved and the downtown area of Vegas had reasonably priced hotels.

For the past fifteen years until this Covid-19 nightmare, I had avoided the loneliness of Christmas by flying to Las Vegas for a week and returning well before New Year's Eve when the prices skyrocketed.

I was an extremely disciplined gambler and enjoyed low denomination slot machines. I had a penchant for numbers and statistics and kept precise track of many things including my losses and individual jackpots.

I decided that Las Vegas would be my next destination. I would leave as soon as the house sold.

As a result of having made a major decision, I slept well on Saturday night.

Sunday was completely uneventful although there was a blizzard which raged most of the day which would have kept me inside anyway.

I moved some of the items from my dining-room office upstairs to the bright blue bedroom. Perhaps I'd get Pete Conrad to help me carry the desk and bookcase up there when I listed the house for sale with him.

It was still too blustery in the evening to bother shoveling the snow off the driveway so I stayed inside and pored over my finances. Besides, the shovel the vendors had left me was a bit small to be particularly effective.

By eleven o'clock I was mentally exhausted so hit the sack.

The next month or two would unveil an entirely new chapter in my life.

Running my own small town legal practice had turned out to be more of a nightmare than a pleasure. At least I'd tried it so would never again be plagued by regrets that I had chosen the wrong career path by working for a law firm.

In the night I had an unsettling dream and woke suddenly.

Strange noises filled the air and in my confusion I wondered what was going on outside.

For a moment I lay there attempting to identify the noises. It sounded like a construction crew was working nearby which didn't make any sense.

Then I heard sirens and realized that an acrid odor had become apparent.

I sat up in bed, my mind still a bit wobbly.

Then it hit me.

My home was on fire.

I leapt out of bed and raced downstairs. The kitchen at the rear of the main floor was in flames which meant that I couldn't escape through the back door.

The front door also appeared to be on fire.

I raced into the dining-room, grabbed my smart phone and my briefcase which held the financial documents I had been working on. My winter coat was hanging on a rack beside the door. I took that coat and my winter boots and ran out the door just as the fire engine screeched to a stop in front of my home.

I ran toward the front sidewalk.

"Is there anyone still inside the house?" a fireman shouted.

"No, I'm the only occupant and I have no pets."

I turned around to discover with horror that my home was now fully engulfed in flames.

As I moved out of the way of the firefighters, I put on my winter boots and coat.

In the minute or two it took me to put on the warm clothes, the roof of my home collapsed in a booming heap.

If I had been a deeper sleeper, I would almost certainly have died in the conflagration.

A police car arrived as did another vehicle with FIRE INSPECTOR emblazoned on the side.

When they learned that I was the homeowner and that I had been in the home alone, the cop decided to take me to the police station where I could stay warm.

The officer assured me that there was nothing I could do here at the property. My legs and feet were beginning to get cold because my pajama bottoms weren't thick and I hadn't been wearing socks in bed. I drove with the cop to the station.

CHAPTER 29 (Investigation)

Once inside the station, I was provided with hot coffee in a small interrogation room. I was also handed a disposable face mask.

About ten minutes later a gentleman entered the room and introduced himself as Detective Moe Enright.

"I understand that you were in the home while it was on fire. Do you have any idea how the fire started?"

"No I don't. I was upstairs asleep when some strange sounds woke me up. For a few moments I couldn't figure out what was causing the noise. It sounded like a construction crew. My brain cleared and I realized that I could smell smoke. I jumped out of bed, grabbed my wallet and keys and ran downstairs. The kitchen was already in flames and the front door area also seemed to be on fire so I exited the house through the dining-room door at the side of the home. I had been using that room as my law office until a few days ago."

"Did you call 911?"

"I never even thought to do that but I could hear sirens so I assumed that help was already on the way. I was in a bit of a panic but I did manage to grab my smart phone, my briefcase and my winter coat and boots from the dining-room office as I left the house."

"Do you mind if I examine those items?"

"Go ahead."

I watched as Enright opened the briefcase and rifled through the papers inside but he didn't ask any questions.

He had me open my smart phone and show him the last numbers I'd called.

"Who were these calls made to?"

I glanced at the list of recent phone numbers.

"One of these is probably Desmond Carlyle, the attorney. The other recent one is to Pete Conrad who is a local realtor. The earlier calls will be business related. I closed my law office up late last week."

"Why did you do that?"

"I had run afoul of a powerful resident and I believed that he would make my life miserable if I remained in Pittsburg."

"Who was that?"

"His name is Johnathan Baxter. We had two run-ins on unrelated legal matters and Baxter was highly displeased with the outcomes."

"He is a big-wig around here."

Just then another fellow walked in the room and introduced himself as Jacob Terpstra, the fire inspector.

"The fire has now been fully extinguished but the house is a total loss. I'm so sorry to have to inform you of the extent of the damage."

"My car is in the detached garage at the rear of the property. Was the garage also destroyed?"

"No, they managed to prevent the fire from spreading either to the garage or to other nearby homes. Do you have any enemies that you're aware of?"

"The only enemy I've encountered is Johnathan Baxter. I'm new to Pittsburg and have only met a handful of people here. Why do you ask?"

"There appears to be some evidence of an accelerant around the front door and definitely all over the rear of the dwelling. This fire was intentionally set. Although it could be a random arsonist who assumed the house was vacant, the fact that you were inside the home when the fire was set is worrisome."

"Is the home insured?" Enright asked.

"Yes it is. I've only lived there since December 24th."

"Did you have any gas cans in the home?"

"No."

"What about in the garage?"

"It was empty when I purchased the house. I hadn't purchased a lawn mower or gas can yet. I was waiting for spring."

"Did you venture out into your back yard yesterday during the snowstorm?"

"No, I stayed in all day. I couldn't even be bothered to shovel the driveway."

"The reason I ask is that there are footprints in the snow which were not made by the fire crew."

"Well, they definitely weren't mine."

"We'll have a more detailed report available in the next day or so. I'm sorry for your loss, sir but at least you're alive."

"The only clothes I've got are the pajamas and winter coat I'm wearing. Will I be able to access my vehicle? I'll need it in order to locate a hotel room and then purchase various things I'll need."

"Some debris will have to be removed from the driveway before you can drive your car out of the garage. That should happen later today."

Terpstra left to return to the fire scene.

Enright delved deeply into my confrontations with Johnathan Baxter. I divulged all the details of both legal files.

"Do you think Mr. Baxter possesses enough animosity toward you to torch your home while you're in in?"

"I have no way of answering that question. Baxter could be a complete sociopath for all I know. Have you been with Pittsburg law enforcement for a while?"

"I've worked in the department for the past twenty-two years."

"In that case you should be able to answer the question about Johnathan Baxter better than I can. I can't be the first resident he's taken a serious dislike to."

"That's an interesting angle. Before I go down that road, I'll have an officer canvass the neighborhood. It's possible that someone noticed a suspicious person in the area of your home."

"The first fire engine arrived just as I was running out of the house. Do you know who called the fire in?"

"No, but I can find out right now."

Enright made a call and a minute or so later had his answer.

"An elderly lady who lives across the street from your house called 911 when she saw flames erupting from your home. That's not a positive sign because it means the arsonist wanted you dead if in fact he knew you were in the house. Have you noticed anyone following you in the past day or two?"

"No."

"I notice in your briefcase that you appeared to have been working on your finances."

"That's correct. I closed up my law practice late last week and had contacted a realtor about listing my home. Last evening I was assessing how much money I'd lost on the law office venture."

"Are you in some kind of financial difficulty?"

"No. In fact I'm quite wealthy."

"I mean no offence, but the area of the city you lived in wasn't the least bit upscale."

"I'm also rather frugal. When I arrived in Pittsburg I quickly discovered that available apartments were scarce because of the local university. I decided to purchase an inexpensive home from which I could also operate my hobby legal practice. I had no need of an income stream but I did require something to fill some of my time."

"Were you an attorney before moving to Pittsburg?"

"Yes I was. My law partners bought me out a week before Christmas and our agreement was that I couldn't practice within 500 miles of our office for a period of five years. It just happened that I was a member of the Kansas Bar Association so I moved here in order to try my hand at operating a small-time law practice."

I purposely didn't divulge that I had been a lawyer in New York State. I still wanted my New York life to be completely separate from my Kansas experience. Tossing in the 500 mile distance saved me from disclosing that the non-competition agreement actually referred to anywhere in New York State.

Enright continued with his queries.

"Why did you choose Pittsburg?"

"It was the right size and from the internet I determined that the climate would be more pleasant than what I was used to back east."

"It's almost five o'clock now. I can drive you to a hotel if you'd like."

"I'd appreciate that, Detective. Can we drive past my property on the way?"

It was both depressing and frightening to see the rubble of my home. One small fire engine was still on site just in case the fire hadn't been totally extinguished. The fire inspector's car was also present.

"The driveway looks to be clear enough that I could remove my vehicle from the garage. That would make today much easier for me."

"I'll ask permission from Jacob Terpstra. You may as well remain in the car where it's warm."

Enright returned a few minutes later.

"Jacob wants to look inside your garage first before he lets you remove the vehicle."

"That's fine. I salvaged my keys before fleeing the fire so I can let him in right now."

Terpstra was quickly satisfied that the garage was empty except for my Hyundai. He did search the vehicle first before giving me the okay to drive it away. I assumed he was looking for a container of gas.

Enright remained at the scene because he wanted to examine the footprints in the snow that Terpstra had mentioned.

I drove to a hotel and booked a room for two nights.

CHAPTER 30 (Sorting Out the Mess)

It was still dark out when I entered my hotel room and suddenly realized that I was exhausted.

I climbed into the bed and tried to recall the series of events beginning at the moment I woke up, but before I knew it, I had drifted off to sleep.

The sound of a vacuum cleaner in the hallway woke me. The bedside clock indicated that it was eleven o'clock.

I showered and then put my pajamas back on.

My first phone call was to my homeowner's insurance agent who advised me that I would have to deal directly with the company. She provided me with the toll free number.

After a brief wait I spoke to a live person and advised the insurance company what had happened to me a few hours earlier.

Since I no longer had access to a printer, the representative made an appointment for me to attend at my insurance agent's office at one o'clock today. An adjuster from the company would meet me there and process my initial claim.

This hotel didn't provide room service so I drove to Wal-Mart and purchased an electric razor, toothbrush, toothpaste and a few clothes.

Back at the hotel I shaved, brushed my teeth and dressed properly.

I phoned Pete Conrad and told him what had just happened. Pete was shocked.

My next stop was a diner where I ate lunch and then drove to my insurance agent's office.

The adjuster's name was Paul Skelding and he was a chap about my age.

Paul opened a file and asked me a few preliminary questions confirming how long I had owned the home and what use I had made of the place. Fortunately I had informed the insurance agent when I bought the home that I intended to use the dining-room as a legal office.

Paul eventually got to more pertinent questions.

"Have they determined how the fire started?"

"Yes they have. It was deliberately set. Evidence of an accelerant was found at the front door and all over the rear portion of the home."

"Were you at home when the fire started?"

"I was asleep upstairs in my bed."

I told Paul about waking up confused, smelling smoke and then running for my life.

"Have the police made any progress in their investigation?"

"I doubt it. The fire inspector did notice footprints in the snow in my backyard and the detective investigating the arson was going to look into those footprints early this morning when he drove me to the property so that I could remove my vehicle from the detached garage which was spared from the flames."

"Your policy indicates that the property was mortgage free."

"That's correct. I paid for the home with cash and didn't require a mortgage."

"Your policy covers you for full replacement of both the building and contents. Do you intend to rebuild?"

"No I don't. In fact I had contacted a realtor a day or two prior to the fire to ascertain how much I should list the place for. I had closed up my legal office and resigned from the Kansas Bar Association last Thursday. My intention was to leave Pittsburg as soon as the house sold."

"Why was that?"

"I had only attracted two clients in the month I had my office open and both of those pitted me against a very influential local resident. He made my life miserable on both of those files by persuading both sets of clients to lodge an ethics complaint against me with the Kansas Bar Association. He also sued me in Small Claims Court in connection with one of the files but we settled that matter on Friday."

"Did you pay him any damages?"

"No, I persuaded his attorney that they were no match for me in court and that I'd humiliate them if they proceeded to trial. They dropped the lawsuit with no payment required. Their claim was beyond ridiculous and the lawyer realized that it was a guaranteed loser."

"Have the ethical complaints been dealt with?"

"They have as far as the Kansas Office of the Disciplinary Administrator is concerned although they ducked out on the second claim when I advised them that I was willing to resign my licence to practice in Kansas since I had no further desire to practice law in this state or elsewhere."

Skelding asked my permission for him to speak with Penelope Crawford and I said that he could but that for privacy reasons she likely wouldn't discuss the matters with him unless he called her now while I was present.

That's what he did.

Penelope was shocked to learn about the fire and was quite forthright with Skelding about the two claims. She stressed that in both cases I had done a remarkable job for the clients although technically it was a violation to loan money to a client without requiring that client to obtain independent legal advice even though I charged no interest.

Skelding was silent for a minute or two after the call ended. Finally he blurted out, "Johnathan Baxter is a formidable opponent."

"My feeling is that if Baxter orchestrated the arson, then my life might still be in danger if I stick around Pittsburg. If he had nothing to do with it, then it was just my bad luck that an arsonist picked my house to torch."

"I'll do what I can to process your claim quickly. The company has a lot of control over the damages. Most decisions aren't left up to you. How much furniture was in the dwelling?"

"The vendors had left some basic items and Pete Conrad probably still has photos of the various rooms to show what furniture was present and his previous listing will show the square footage of the home. The only furniture items I purchased were an antique desk and matching bookcase for which I paid $1,500 but I also bought a printer and some office supplies. I hadn't yet purchased a TV. My desktop computer and most of my clothes were also destroyed in the fire although I managed to rescue my smart phone on my way out the door."

"What are your thoughts regarding a cash payout for your total claim? Arriving at a mutually acceptable figure would allow you to wash your hands of the property immediately. That would permit you to avoid being forced to rebuild."

"I'm quite well-to-do and certainly have no intention of milking this fire to enrich myself. I paid $45,000 for the place and Pete Conrad suggested that I list it for $52,900. The décor was hideous to most folks although personally I loved the vibrant colors. You'll see what I mean when you look at Pete's prior listing photos. I was going to include the furniture in the sale with the possible exception of the desk and bookcase. What total figure would the insurance company be happy with?"

"Let me examine Pete Conrad's listing first and I'll get back to you. From what you've told me, I expect that the company might pay a lump sum of

$60,000 and take a Deed of your property."

"I'd be satisfied with that amount because it would allow me to leave Pittsburg in the next couple of days."

"Can you meet me back here at four o'clock? I'll try to have an answer for you by then."

"I look forward to our next meeting, Paul. Thank you for being so accommodating."

CHAPTER 31 (On the Road Again)

I went back to my hotel to wait for the next meeting and to fill in the list of the items I lost in the fire.

It wasn't easy trying to remember how many business suits, ties, sweaters and other clothing items I owned.

My insurance agent had provided a copy of my policy for me and I read it over so that I'd have a better idea of what other losses I could claim. For example my hotel accommodation was covered.

When I returned to meet Paul, he had been an industrious boy. In addition to visiting Pete Conrad, Paul had spoken with the fire inspector and with Detective Enright before calling his boss at the insurance company.

I handed Paul the preliminary list of my belongings destroyed in the fire and he examined it carefully before we got down to detailed negotiations.

"If I understand you correctly, you would be amenable to accepting a lump sum in full satisfaction of all your losses and that a quick settlement is preferable so that you can leave Pittsburg as soon as possible."

"That's correct, Paul."

"I've spoken with the insurance company representative and they're willing to offer you the lump sum of $60,000 and accept a Deed of your property."

"I'd be happy with that lump sum in the circumstances. As I mentioned, the furniture was worthless to me. Also, I no longer have any reason to own eight or nine business suits since I intend to retire fully."

"In that case we have a deal. The various release documents can be ready tomorrow and our local attorney can prepare the Deed."

We arranged to meet at their lawyer's office tomorrow at eleven o'clock.

I was quite relieved as I picked up my supper at a fast food drive-thru and took my meal back to the hotel.

The settlement suited me perfectly and the insurance company saved itself tens of thousands of dollars in the process. It was no surprise that they had jumped at the chance to settle the claim quickly.

I remained in my hotel room all evening just in case Baxter had hired a hit man to take me out once he learned that I hadn't perished in the fire.

On Tuesday morning I checked out of my hotel at nine-thirty and then stopped at a fast food outlet for breakfast before driving to the lawyer's office.

The documents were ready for execution.

I signed them including the Deed and the lawyer handed me a bank draft in the amount of $60,000.

I deposited the draft into my checking account at my bank and withdrew ample cash to last me during my excursion to Las Vegas.

Before leaving town, I phoned Detective Enright. They were following a lead regarding the footprints in the snow but really had made no headway yet in their investigation of the arson.

Enright had my smart phone number in case he needed to contact me. I told him that I hadn't yet decided where to make my next home.

At one-thirty I drove south out of Pittsburg on Highway 69 and within half an hour I had entered Oklahoma.

The Kansas portion of my life was over.

I hadn't bothered to phone Candace Blake or Harold and Joan Els. They had forfeited the right to know my affairs.

For obvious reasons I hadn't called Johnathan Baxter or Desmond Carlyle either.

In fact, in order to reduce the opportunity for Baxter to track me down, I now intended to go back to using my former name Carl Saunders.

I'd never gotten comfortable answering to the name Donald and in fact switching to Donald had turned out to be extremely unlucky for me.

When Highway 69 intersected Highway 60, I veered west.

I hadn't travelled on that highway for thirty minutes when I was hit by some sort of panic attack.

I pulled off onto the shoulder of the road and started hyperventilating.

Nothing like this had ever happened to me. At first I thought that perhaps I was having a heart attack or stroke but quickly figured out that it was a delayed reaction to having almost died in the fire.

Up until now I had shrugged off my brush with death but clearly the event had impacted me far more deeply than I had realized.

Eventually I calmed down and resumed driving.

When I reached Bartlesville I almost stopped for the night but something deep inside my psyche urged me to put more distance between myself and the danger in Pittsburg. I continued driving until just after dark and found a hotel in Ponca City.

This hotel had its own diner so I had supper there and then studied maps back in my room.

For the next three days I drove mostly on Interstate 40 from early morning until shortly after dark.

Late on Friday afternoon I finally arrived in Las Vegas, Nevada.

I found a hotel room at the Four Queens in the downtown section of the city and paid for the room for two nights.

The next portion of my life had begun.

CHAPTER 32 (Getting my Bearings)

I ate supper in Magnolia's in the casino section of the Four Queens and treated myself to a delicious fish dinner and two large mugs of dark draft beer.

Fortunately I hadn't experienced another panic attack and hoped that the trauma of the fire had now been relegated to a distant memory.

I returned to my room after supper. The long drive had tired me out and I had no desire to gamble tonight.

There was a lovely high-rise condominium building called The Ogden directly across the street from the El Cortez Hotel and Casino two blocks east of the Four Queens.

I checked on the internet. Quite a few units were shown as being for rent starting at $1,695 per month. Several apartments were also for sale ranging from $276,900 and up.

Tomorrow I'd wander over to the building and determine if in fact there were some apartments for rent.

Renting would be somewhat preferable to buying just in case I didn't enjoy residing in Las Vegas after all. Having said that however, the monthly cost of owning a unit would be substantially less than the rent I would be forced to pay.

I slept soundly and on Saturday morning I ate a full breakfast in Magnolia's.

After breakfast I walked over to The Ogden.

A pleasant lady named Faith showed me a list of which units were available to rent and to purchase. The building had been completely sold out and the apartments for sale were all resales by existing owners.

There were no realtors on site to show me any of the available units but Faith mentioned that there was a notice on the main bulletin board by an owner who had one of his units for rent.

I phoned the number on the notice.

A gentleman answered.

"Good morning, sir. My name is Carl Saunders. I'm in the main lobby of The Ogden and the lady at the sales office directed me to your notice on the bulletin board. I just arrived in Las Vegas yesterday and I'm staying at the Four Queens while I look for an apartment to rent."

"Where are you from, Carl?"

"I'm a recently retired lawyer from Buffalo, New York."

"I'm also a retired attorney. My name is Mike Black. I'll come right down and speak with you in person."

Mike exited the elevator a few minutes later. He looked quite a bit like me, tall with white hair and a slim build.

"Have you been to Las Vegas before now?" Mike asked.

"I've been coming here for the past fifteen years during the Christmas week. I'm long ago divorced with no kids and Las Vegas is a great spot at which to escape what for most folks is a time for family celebration. Nobody notices a guy on his own. Where did you have your law practice?"

"I worked for a large firm in San Diego and also used to visit Las Vegas on a regular basis. I bought two units in this building in early 2009 when prices were at rock bottom. I live in a two-bedroom apartment and rent out the one-bedroom unit. I'm also divorced."

Mike invited me up to see the vacant furnished apartment and mentioned that both of his units were on the ninth floor.

We chatted about our respective legal careers. Mike had been retired for two years. I told him how my partners had booted me out of my firm with about thirty minutes notice.

"I'm not surprised, Carl. Loyalty has been a complete no-show in our profession for a long time now."

We bonded quite quickly and within an hour I had rented the one-bedroom apartment for $1,750 per month which included utilities and one parking spot.

Mike was very accommodating and we agreed to a month-to-month tenancy wherein either of us could terminate the tenancy on sixty days' notice.

I paid Mike $1,050 in cash to cover the balance of February and I wrote a check to him for the full March rent. He handed me the keys and suddenly I had a place to live.

We also arranged to have supper together later on.

CHAPTER 33 (A New Friend)

I went back to my hotel and relaxed for a couple of hours. My innate frugality wanted to use the room for at least a little while today since I had already paid for tonight.

Finally at four o'clock I checked out of the hotel and drove to my new home at The Ogden.

It was sad how few possessions I currently owned. I'd worn the same clothes during the entire four day drive. Tomorrow I needed to hit a department store and purchase whatever items I would need to sustain me over the next little while.

Mike knocked on my door at six as we had arranged and we headed across the street to the El Cortez to have supper there.

We each requested a large draft beer before placing our food order.

"Have you moved your belongings in to the apartment yet?" Mike inquired.

"I did but at the moment I own practically nothing."

"Why is that?"

"I've gone through a rather nasty adventure since getting turfed out of my law practice."

"What sort of adventure are you talking about?"

I explained to Mike the background which led to my being licensed to practice law in the state of Kansas.

"I'd always fantasized about operating my own small town legal practice so I purchased a modest home in the city of Pittsburg in southeast Kansas and decided to use the dining-room as my law office. The purchase closed the day before Christmas."

"I assume the experiment didn't pan out."

"That's an understatement."

I proceeded to tell Mike about the two clients I did manage to attract and the treachery that followed.

"That was a nasty adventure," Mike commented.

"That was bad enough but then the situation took a terrible turn for the worse. Early this past Monday morning I woke up to strange sounds and the smell of smoke. My home was on fire. I managed to escape in my pajamas and winter coat but all I could grab on my way out was my wallet, smart phone and briefcase. It was a definite case of arson."

"That's awful."

"I came to a quick settlement with the insurance company and left Pittsburg the following day. If

Johnathan Baxter was the force behind the arson, then I was concerned that he might hire a hit man to finish the job. All I've purchased so far is a razor, toothbrush and a few items of clothing. Tomorrow or Monday I'll hit some stores and replenish my wardrobe."

"Have the police made any headway in their investigation?"

"I don't know. The detective handling the case has my smart phone number and email address but hasn't contacted me yet."

Mike wanted to know how I had managed to settle so quickly with the insurance company. I explained that it was mutually beneficial. They paid off the claim cheaply by avoiding replacement value issues but I still got fully compensated for what I had actually spent on my home and contents.

Eventually we changed the topic of conversation and shared stories about our days in practice.

It was nice to have someone my own age and with a similar background to talk with.

By the end of the meal I knew that I had made my first friend here in Las Vegas.

CHAPTER 34 (Startling Developments)

On Sunday which was also Valentine's Day, I went shopping and purchased two suits, some shoes and various other clothes.

I also bought a desktop computer and a small printer.

On Monday I made the necessary arrangements to have internet service and by that evening I was hooked up and began browsing.

The Pittsburg newspaper had run a couple of articles about the fire including a photo of the rubble. The reporter had learned from the fire inspector that it was definitely arson but the police refused to release any details about their investigation other than to emphasize that the occupant of the home was not a suspect and in fact had been fortunate to narrowly escape the blaze when he woke up to the smell of smoke and the sound of the crumbling structure.

On Wednesday afternoon I received a phone call from Detective Enright.

After confirming that it was really me, Enright hit me with some stunning news.

"I followed the footprints in the snow out your back yard and into the property behind yours. They seemed to stop abruptly on the street a block away so we assumed that the arsonist got in a vehicle and drove off. We thought the trail had gone cold at that point but we got lucky."

Enright paused for effect before continuing.

"A nosy neighbor with insomnia happened to notice a strange van parked outside her home in the middle of the night. She put on her coat and went out to investigate because overnight parking isn't allowed on that street. The van was empty but she wrote down the license plate number. It took us a few days before we canvassed her neighborhood but we tracked down the owner of the vehicle. Then good things began to happen."

Again Enright went quiet for a moment.

"I'm all ears, Detective."

"The fellow who owned the vehicle still had the gas can in his possession as well as some unregistered firearms and illegal drugs. We seized the available evidence and brought the chap in for questioning. He confessed to starting the fire."

"I'm pleased to hear that. Was it just a random act of vandalism that made him choose my house?"

"I'm not done with the good news. He was paid to torch your home by none other than Johnathan Baxter himself."

"That's dreadful. The bastard was trying to kill me after all."

"That's how it seems. The arsonist has been charged with numerous offences but the District Attorney hasn't decided yet whether there is enough evidence even to arrest Johnathan Baxter let alone charge him with conspiracy to commit arson. That's where you come in."

"I'm not following you."

"If the DA charges Baxter then she'll want you to appear as a witness at his preliminary hearing in order to show motive for the arson."

"I'm living in Las Vegas now. Returning to Pittsburg isn't on my bucket list."

"The DA's name is Valerie Brewster. I'll have her give you a call and discuss the matter."

We ended the call and I mulled over what Enright had told me. Air travel was too risky because of mandatory Covid-19 tests and potential quarantine periods. If my presence was required, then I'd either have to drive there and back or take the bus and then rent a car.

Neither option was attractive.

CHAPTER 35 (Money Talks)

On Friday Valerie Brewster, the District Attorney phoned from her Crawford County office in Girard.

We spent the first twenty minutes discussing my various run-ins with Johnathan Baxter wherein I explained my role as attorney in connection with Joan and Harold Els' file and also regarding Brady Mackintosh.

I restricted the information I divulged to the legal proceedings only.

"Let's begin with Mr. Baxter's threat to you after the Mackintosh court hearing. Did anyone else hear Baxter utter his threat?"

"He and I were alone at the time."

"If there is no corroboration, then Baxter will simply deny that he threatened you. If fact, he didn't indicate in any manner than he would physically harm you."

"That's true, Ms. Brewster. I did mention the conversation immediately after it occurred to Candace Blake, a lady who accompanied me to the courtroom that day."

"Will she back up your claim?"

"She might not. When I received notice of Brady Mackintosh's complaint to the Kansas Office of the

Disciplinary Administrator, I phoned Candace to ascertain why her friend's son was suddenly turning on me. Candace was curt with me but did disclose that Brady had reconciled with Baxter's granddaughter, Amy. Candace refused to get further involved because Baxter had some leverage over her mother. Candace told me not to call her again."

"But you said that it was Candace Blake who contacted you to represent Brady."

"I know. Candace was thrilled with the results of the court hearing but that all changed after Brady made his complaint and Johnathan Baxter sued me in Small Claims Court."

"Do you think Baxter bought off Brady?"

"I fully expect that he did but I can't prove it."

"At least I can contact Candace and Brady and ask them. If they refuse to confirm your version of events, then my hands are tied."

"That's fair enough."

"That brings us to the file with Harold and Joan Els. Why do you think they turned on you?"

"They told me why and I supported their decision, but since the conversation involved our relationship as attorney and client, then I'm not willing to divulge the details. It's possible that they might open up if you contact them."

"If they don't, then all I've got is your word against Baxter's."

"That's life in the criminal justice system as I'm sure you're fully aware. Isn't your best evidence against Johnathan the testimony of the arsonist?"

"It is but the chap has lawyered up and now refuses to speak with us. In fact he has just recanted his earlier statements that Johnathan Baxter hired him to torch your home. His confession didn't contain any information about Baxter other than admitting that Baxter hired him."

"It looks to me as if Baxter has already bought his way out of trouble. Dragging me to Pittsburg won't bolster your case."

"I'll get back to you. At the very least I want to speak with your former clients as well as Candace Blake before I make any decision."

We ended the call.

I sat back and evaluated the situation.

It was disgusting how money could subvert justice.

One possible way to make Baxter suffer for his indiscretions came to mind. Hitting Baxter in the pocketbook was likely the only punishment available.

I phoned Paul Skelding, the insurance adjuster who had handled my claim.

"Hello Paul. I've recently been called by Detective Enright and just now by the District Attorney of the County of Crawford."

I filled Paul in on the recent developments, all of which were news to him. Apparently nothing had been printed in the newspapers.

"The reason for this call is to apprise you of the situation just in case your company wishes to recover your insurance losses from Johnathan Baxter. The state probably can't prove Baxter's guilt in the arson beyond a reasonable doubt but you only have to show his involvement on a balance of probabilities."

"I appreciate the phone call, Mr. Saunders. I'll take it up with my bosses and proceed accordingly. Have you gotten your own life back together?"

"I believe so. I had one panic attack on my drive here to Las Vegas but since then I've coped well. I'd appreciate a call at some point letting me know whether your employer is going to pursue Baxter for the insurance losses."

“I’ll do that. Thanks for the follow-up call and best of luck in your new home.”

There, at least I’d done something to get back at Johnathan Baxter.

CHAPTER 36 (Long Trip)

Life went on.

I was quite happy. Mike Black and I had become close friends and shared meals at various downtown restaurants at least three times a week.

Gambling wasn't much fun yet because of the mandatory masks so I only played the slots occasionally.

No one had called me from Pittsburg so I assumed that there had been no progress in the cases against the arsonist or Johnathan Baxter.

The Pittsburg newspaper made no mention of the cases although the on-line version probably contained only a small portion of the news available in the print edition.

On the last day of March the District Attorney finally called me but the news was mixed.

The state had decided after all to charge Johnathan Baxter with conspiracy to commit arson but the local paper had refused to name Baxter at this early stage of the process.

That was the positive portion of the phone call.

The decidedly negative part was that my presence was required at Baxter's preliminary hearing which was to begin on Wednesday, the 7th of April which was only a week away.

I checked out the bus schedules but decided that the long ordeal on a smelly bus would be torture.

As much as I loathed the idea, driving to Pittsburg was my least horrible option.

I packed one black suit and some casual clothes and left on my journey early Friday morning.

At this time of year it was wise to stick to the interstate highways until I'd crossed over the various mountain ranges.

Interstate 70 through Utah and Colorado was still too treacherous because of snowstorms in the higher elevations, so I opted to take Interstate 40.

I drove about 500 miles and finally after eight and a half hours I took a hotel room in Albuquerque, New Mexico. I had been lucky with today's weather and only encountered two small patches of rain or wet snow.

On Saturday I again started out early and eventually tired out late in the afternoon and found a motel in Clinton, Oklahoma.

Sunday was a miserable day on the highway with constant rain, heavy at times.

By the time I reached Coffeyville, Kansas my eyes felt and looked like bloodshot lead weights so I took a motel room there.

Tomorrow I'd find a motel in Pittsburg and book it for a few nights.

I slept for twelve solid hours and woke up at ten o'clock on Monday morning. My eyes were still sore.

After checking out of the motel, I drove to Pittsburg and found a room at the Holiday Lodge, the same place I'd stayed when I first arrived in Pittsburg last December. I decided to book the room one day at a time just in case the hearing was cancelled or wrapped up early.

Then I ate lunch at a downtown diner.

For this brief stay in Kansas, I would again be Donald Saunders rather than Carl Saunders.

CHAPTER 37 (Unwelcome)

After lunch I drove past my former home. The rubble had been fully cleared away and there was a BUILDING LOT FOR SALE sign pounded into the ground.

From my motel I phoned Paul Skelding who was surprisingly evasive.

When I asked him if the insurance company had received any offers yet on my property, he merely replied that his company no longer owned the land and refused to answer my other queries regarding Johnathan Baxter or how the company had managed to sell the land so quickly.

When I mentioned that he was being cryptic, Paul replied that the company had sold the land and closed their file but that any details were confidential. He did admit that the company had recovered all their losses. That pleased me.

I drove to Pete Conrad's real estate office.

Pete was working but was not pleased to see me. The only information I gleaned from him was that one of Baxter's companies now owned my former property and that the vacant land was now listed for $24,000. Pete gave me the brush-off by saying that he had to rush off to a showing.

Somewhat confused by the negative reception from folks who had once been friendly, I returned to my motel and phoned Detective Enright.

He took my call but seemed to be completely in the dark about the ownership changes of my former property.

"The city seems to have rallied behind Johnathan Baxter," Moe explained. "He has a ton of friends in Pittsburg and news of his arrest just became public on Saturday. I'm afraid that you won't be well received around here."

"That's good to know. I guess I'd better call Valerie Brewster and advise her that I'm in the area."

I wasn't able to reach Brewster but her assistant made an appointment for me to see the DA tomorrow afternoon at two o'clock.

For supper I went to the steak house where I had shared a meal with Candace before she turned on me.

I was just finishing my meal when Desmond Carlyle entered the establishment. He glared at me but didn't approach my table.

After supper I returned to my motel and remained there.

On Tuesday morning I checked out and drove to Fort Scott about thirty miles to the north and booked a hotel room for tonight only. I didn't feel comfortable in Pittsburg.

I ate lunch in Fort Scott and then drove to Girard for my meeting with Valerie Brewster.

Even she seemed uncomfortable being in my presence. She informed me of the questions she would likely ask me at tomorrow's preliminary hearing.

Her proposed questions were rather superficial and I got the distinct impression that her heart wasn't in this prosecution.

My best guess was that Brewster had caved to the pressure from Baxter and his many supporters.

Since I was in Girard anyway, I dropped in to the land registry office and discovered that my former home had been sold by my insurance company to Baxter's numbered company for $63,000.

I drove back to my hotel in Fort Scott after stopping to purchase a submarine sandwich which I ate later in my room.

It had been a waste of time coming back to Kansas.

CHAPTER 38 (Surprises)

On Wednesday morning I checked out of my hotel in Fort Scott and drove to Girard.

I felt quite unpopular.

First I had been discarded like a used condom by my own law firm in Buffalo and now the Crawford County folks were treating me like unwanted rubbish.

If the preliminary hearing wrapped up today, then I wasn't remaining in Kansas. I'd drive to Oklahoma and spend the night as far away from Pittsburg as possible.

As a witness I was shunted into a small room by myself since I wasn't permitted to hear testimony from any prior witnesses.

At noon a sandwich and small container of apple juice were brought in to me.

Finally at two-thirty someone arrived and escorted me into the courtroom where I was sworn in and took the witness stand.

Johnathan Baxter was in court dressed in a very expensive suit. Desmond Carlyle was also present but an extremely distinguished attorney named

Edward Kafka from Wichita was handling Baxter's defense.

Valerie Brewster asked me her questions about my involvement with Johnathan Baxter prior to the house fire.

I answered honestly and was fully cognizant of the fact that she avoided pressing me about the ethics complaints filed by my only two clients.

It was obvious to me that Brewster was purposely fluffing the prosecution.

Baxter was pleased with the examination in chief because he wore a satisfied smirk once Brewster advised the court that she had no further questions.

Kafka stood up to cross-examine me.

"Did I understand correctly that those two files were the only times you had any contact with Mr. Baxter."

"That's correct."

"On the Els' mortgage matter, all you did was pay off in full the mortgage Mr. Baxter held from Mr. and Mrs. Els. It seems that in fact you did my client a favor by saving him the cost and headache of foreclosing on the elderly couple."

"That's true unless Mr. Baxter's intention was to gain ownership of the one piece of property in that general location which had eluded him. He did purchase the mortgage at full face value and then promptly hit the borrowers with the demand that they pay him in full in thirty days. I'll let you connect the dots."

"Harold and Joan Els have already testified on the matter. They claim that you took advantage of them by purchasing their mortgage from Mr. Baxter."

"How could they possibly come to that conclusion? I bailed them out of their financial crisis by loaning them the funds they required and charged no interest on the loan. That was clearly of huge benefit to them."

"That's not the way they view your involvement. They view you as a crook who tried to steal their land from them. Why do you think that is?"

"Didn't you ask them?"

"I did but now I'm asking you."

"You might not like the answer."

The Judge intervened.

"Answer the question, Mr. Saunders."

"There is an element of client confidentiality, Judge. I do believe however that their rights have been waived since they apparently have maligned my involvement in their financial and legal affairs. If you concur, then I'll be pleased to answer the question posed by Mr. Kafka."

"Go ahead. I'll stop you if I believe that the circumstances warrant it."

"I paid off the Els' mortgage and tax arrears on January 7th, the day they first contacted me and thereafter began handling an insurance claim on Harold's behalf. On the Saturday morning of January 30th they came to my office without an appointment. They were in a quandary. A man had come to their home the previous evening. If they switched attorneys and complained about me to the Kansas Bar Association, then their promissory note to me would be paid off in full, they would be guaranteed a minimum disability insurance award of $135,000 and their son Dexter would be released from jail. I told them to take the deal because I was a sinking ship now that Johnathan Baxter had decided to demonstrate that I had crossed the wrong man."

This time it was the Judge who asked me a question.

"Were you in fact paid off in full, Mr. Saunders?"

"Yes I was, Judge. On Sunday the very next day I was contacted by a Wichita law firm. I agreed to transfer the file to them immediately and I provided them with the payout amount of Harold and Joan's debt to me. On Monday an attorney with the firm came to my office, handed me the payout check and took over the insurance claim. I provided that firm with a report letter detailing my complete involvement with Mr. and Mrs. Els. By the way, the only legal fee I charged was retaining $1,500 of a $5,000 cost award from the insurance company's attorneys. I remitted the remaining $3,500 directly to Harold and Joan so that they would have some cash to sustain them while I dealt with Harold's insurance claim. Does that sound like I took advantage of them in any way?"

"Mr. Kafka, in light of this testimony, I'm going to recall Harold and Joan Els to the stand after your cross-examination of Mr. Saunders is completed."

Kafka turned his attention back to me.

"That's a fascinating story, Mr. Saunders. But do you have any evidence whatsoever that the source of those funds came from Johnathan Baxter?"

"I do not although it shouldn't be too difficult to trace the funds through the Wichita legal firm. I'm sure that they must know who hired them and where the funds they received actually came from."

Kafka appeared flustered although he was doing his best not to show it.

"I have no further questions for this witness."

"Don't you want to ask me about the other confrontation with Johnathan Baxter over his firing of his granddaughter's boyfriend? That's where the bulk of his animosity toward me arose."

"What part of no further questions don't you comprehend?" Kafka snapped.

Valerie Brewster should have stood up at that point and demanded to examine me about that episode but she sat at her table like a lump of coal.

Even the Judge was surprised.

"Does the prosecution wish to re-examine this witness, Ms. Brewster?"

"We do not, Judge."

"In that case I wish to call Harold and Joan Els back to testify."

The security guard went out to find the old couple.

Baxter was no longer smirking but it was clear from his expression that I wouldn't make his Christmas card list this year.

The guard returned.

"Mr. and Mrs. Els have already left to return home, Judge Carrino."

"That's a shame. We'll have to re-examine them tomorrow. Do you have any other witnesses to call today, Ms. Brewster?"

"No we don't. Donald Saunders and Curtis Jackson were the prosecution's only witnesses."

I knew from the newspaper that Curtis Jackson was the low-life who torched my home with me in it.

"In that case, we'll adjourn until tomorrow morning at ten o'clock," Judge Alice Carrino ordered.

CHAPTER 39 (Motive Established)

I approached Valerie Brewster who didn't seem pleased with me.

"Why didn't you use that golden opportunity that Kafka handed you to grill me about the Brady Mackintosh matter?"

Brewster's face mask inadvertently slipped down below her chin and I notice that my accusation had made her blush.

"I never ask questions of a witness unless I'm relatively certain about what that witness would say."

"But you and I had discussed that matter in great detail. You were fully aware of my allegations regarding Brady Mackintosh."

"I'd suggest that you leave trial strategy up to me, Mr. Saunders."

"What did Curtis Jackson say when you had him on the stand?"

"He refused to say anything other than that his previous statement that Johnathan Baxter had hired him to set fire to your home was a lie."

"Haven't you been able to track the payment Jackson got back to the source?"

"No we haven't. It was made in cash."

"Did you at least enter as evidence Jackson's original confession?"

"We tried but the defence objected. Judge Carrino has reserved judgement on whether it can be admitted into evidence."

Brewster packed up her briefcase and scampered out of the courtroom.

I followed her and then drove straight back to Fort Scott although I made sure that no one was following me.

It seemed to me that Baxter was going to successfully get the charges dropped.

Brewster was doing as little as possible to establish Baxter's guilt.

Small town corruption disgusted me. Underhanded shenanigans were even more rampant in Crawford County than they had been in Buffalo.

In order not to be visible, I got my supper at a drive-thru fast food outlet and ate the food in my vehicle.

Then I got a room at a different hotel in Fort Scott.

On Thursday morning I ate a continental breakfast in my hotel lobby and returned to Girard.

Although the public wasn't permitted in the courtroom during a preliminary hearing, I was allowed to enter because the upcoming testimony by Harold and Joan Els could refute my own statements in which case I would be brought back onto the witness stand to be re-examined on any discrepancies.

To both my and Judge Carrino's surprise, Valerie Brewster stood up and said that she had no questions to pose to Harold or Joan Els.

Kafka rose and said that he also had no questions of either witness.

Judge Carrino pondered this development for a moment before announcing that she had some questions.

Kafka objected but Carrino denied his request.

"Mr. Els, the testimony of Donald Saunders yesterday greatly conflicted with your testimony and that of your wife. Mr. Saunders believes that you received substantial compensation in return for your ethics complaint against Mr. Saunders. Do you care to comment?"

"I need to speak with my wife in private first."

"We'll take a five minute recess while you discuss the matter with Mrs. Els in the back corner of this courtroom where you won't be overheard."

Harold stepped down from the witness box and walked to the rear of the courtroom where Joan joined him.

A few minutes later Harold returned to the witness box.

I was relieved to think that Harold and Joan might tell the truth after all.

Harold rattled off the whole scenario and admitted that he and Joan were afraid to divulge the details of the large payment they received because their son Dexter had been released on parole a few days after they made the ethics complaint against me. They were concerned that whoever had pulled the strings to get Dexter released early could have him dragged back to prison.

It was quite moving testimony.

Joan was sworn in again and confirmed everything that Harold had said.

"Does the prosecution or the defense have any questions for either of these witnesses?"

District Attorney Valerie Brewster did not but Edward Kafka had one question to pose to each witness.

"Do you have any evidence that the money and other benefits you received came from Johnathan Baxter?"

Both Harold and Joan responded that they didn't know for sure where the money had come from. They were just glad to receive the funds and to get their son released from prison early.

Joan added a nice compliment.

"Mr. Saunders turned out to be the most kind and generous attorney we've ever heard of. He bailed us out of a terrible jam where we were certain to lose our home and then he fought the insurance company on our behalf. We're embarrassed now that we disparaged Mr. Saunders here in the courtroom. He is a saint and we treated him terribly. The fact that he almost died in that house fire gives us nightmares."

Judge Carrino dismissed the witnesses and sat in silence for several minutes.

"I require Donald Saunders to return to the witness stand," she ordered.

I stood up and was sworn in again.

"District Attorney Brewster, this court wants to hear more details of the second legal file regarding Brady Mackintosh. Either you can make inquiries of Mr. Saunders or I will."

Brewster demonstrated to my satisfaction that Baxter had somehow coerced her into botching the prosecution. She had no questions.

Kafka stood up and objected to the Judge taking over the prosecution of the case.

Carrino overruled his objection.

"Describe the situation regarding your representation of Brady Mackintosh," she demanded.

I complied by describing everything that occurred from the moment Candace Blake first phoned my office, the court hearing itself, Johnathan Baxter's threat after the hearing, Brady's receipt of the severance funds from me and the relief that Brady's mother, Candace and Brady himself all felt.

Then I told the court about the email from Claudia Norman, Candace's fear that Johnathan Baxter would harm her mother if she continued to support me, the Small Claims Court lawsuit filed against me by Baxter and the resulting animosity between us.

When I was done, Kafka asked me just one question.

"Do you have any evidence whatsoever that Johnathan Baxter had any involvement with the arson at your home?"

"No I don't."

"Are there any further witnesses to be called?"

Both attorneys advised that there were none.

"I'm going to reserve my judgement until tomorrow morning at nine o'clock. I need to examine the precedents regarding admissibility of recanted confession evidence. I want all attorneys present tomorrow as well as Donald Saunders and the accused. Court is adjourned for the day."

CHAPTER 40 (Courtroom Terror)

I was aware of Johnathan Baxter glaring at me as I stood up and exited the courtroom. His face mask hid his facial expression but his eyes showed his hatred of me.

At that moment I was convinced that Baxter had in fact hired the arsonist with the intent to burn me to a crisp.

Rather than return to Fort Scott, I drove east into Missouri and found a hotel room in the small city of Nevada which was about eighteen miles east of Fort Scott. Again I made sure that no one had followed me.

I walked to a nearby diner and had supper and two mugs of beer after which I remained in my hotel room.

On Friday morning I woke early, checked out of my hotel and made it to Girard well before nine o'clock.

I was damn nervous. In addition to my face mask, I also wore a wool toque which completely hid my white hair. I believed in the pit of my stomach that it was prudent to enter the courthouse anonymously just in case Baxter wanted to punish me for complicating his legal defense.

As soon as I got inside the courthouse a few minutes before nine o'clock, I took the stairs up to the courtroom instead of using the elevator.

When I got to the correct floor, I removed my toque and coat and walked into the corridor and quickly to the courtroom.

In Buffalo the court houses had been heavily fortified and guarded with metal detectors and armed security.

In this tiny Kansas county seat none of that was evident. There wasn't even a security guard in the main entrance area.

Kafka and Carlyle were present with Johnathan Baxter at the defense table. Valerie Brewster was also at her prosecutor's table. I took a seat a few rows behind Brewster.

Judge Carrino entered the courtroom accompanied by the court stenographer. We all rose as she walked up to the bench.

She instructed us to be seated.

As had happened on the previous two days, all of us were wearing our face masks even when we were testifying up on the stand. It was beyond ridiculous.

"Does either the defense or prosecution have any comments before I announce my decision regarding the admissibility of Curtis Jackson's recorded interrogation and alleged confession?"

Both Brewster and Kafka replied that they did not.

"In that case my ruling is that those pieces of evidence are admissible at trial. The credibility issue can be dealt with by the respective attorneys at that time."

It sounded to me like Carrino was clearly going to rule that there was sufficient evidence to justify a trial. She had certainly implied that.

"As far as my decision as to whether the prosecution has presented sufficient evidence at this preliminary hearing to warrant a trial, it is my ruling that…"

That was as far as she got.

An armed and masked man burst into the courtroom.

"I want everyone to stand together," he demanded as he waved his gun in the air.

We all obeyed.

My mind was racing while trying to connect the dots. This had to be Johnathan Baxter's doing. I had learned that Curtis Jackson had been released on bail. It seemed unlikely that Baxter would have been able to hire a hit man so quickly. My best guess was that this gunman was Curtis Jackson.

"Which one of you is Donald Saunders?" the gunman inquired.

I decided to test out my theory. I had nothing to lose.

I ripped off my face mask.

"That would be me, Curtis."

The moron took the bait.

"How did you know it was me?"

"I'm not as dumb as I look. Why didn't you kill me before I walked in the court house?"

"That's what Mr. Baxter told me to do but I didn't see you go in."

"That's because I was wearing a toque to hide my white hair and a mask to hide my face. I suspected that Johnathan Baxter might try to silence me so I didn't take any chances that I'd be recognized."

"Now what am I going to do? I don't want to kill everyone."

"Your options are very limited, Curtis. Putting down your gun would be the most sensible choice."

"I don't want to go to jail. I wish I'd never listened to Mr. Baxter in the first place but he had proof that I'd had sex with my thirteen year old girlfriend and threatened to rat me out to the cops if I didn't burn your house down."

I had no idea how to respond.

When in doubt, keep your lip zipped. That was a basic tenet of successful litigation.

Curtis clearly was struggling with his decision and unfortunately didn't appear to have enough brain cells to come to a sensible conclusion.

He stuck the gun in his mouth and I expected Curtis to blow his brains out right in front of us, but he changed his mind and removed the weapon from his mouth.

Curtis aimed the gun at my face.

I closed my eyes.

The sound of a gunshot reverberated in the room but I didn't feel anything.

I opened my eyes just as Curtis inserted the gun back into his mouth and pulled the trigger.

It was a horrible spectacle.

My eyes were glued to the young moron's corpse and I was oblivious to the sounds around me.

I looked down at my shirt to see if I had been shot after all but I appeared to be unharmed.

Still in shock, I watched as a security guard burst into the courtroom.

Someone took hold of my arm and spoke to me.

I didn't register the individual words but turned my head to see who was addressing me.

It was Judge Carrino.

"Are you hurt, Mr. Saunders?"

I understood that comment.

"I don't seem to have been shot. I had my eyes closed when Curtis aimed his gun at my face. Did his first shot miss me?"

"He shot Johnathan Baxter instead of you."

I turned to my other side.

Johnathan Baxter was on the floor with a huge bloody hole in his face. It was absolutely gruesome.

Carrino and her stenographer led me over to the spectators' benches where I sat down to compose myself.

The thought struck me that the two women were reacting to the shootings much more bravely than I was.

But then I was much older.

"I may be a discarded old lawyer, but I'm not dead yet," I remarked to no one in particular at which point I erupted in a gale of laughter.

I must have fainted from the shock at that point.

The next thing I knew I was laying on a sofa and a paramedic was hovering over me.

CHAPTER 41 (Las Vegas Bound)

My faculties quickly returned.

The paramedic was just about to jab me with a needle.

"I'm okay now. I don't need whatever shit is in that needle."

"Are you certain, sir? This is a sedative to help you deal with the shock of the trauma you experienced."

I sat up.

"The Judge and her stenographer handled the situation much better than I did. Was anyone hurt other than the shooter and Johnathan Baxter?"

"Everyone else was unharmed, sir. You're the only one who required any medical attention. The shooter and Mr. Baxter were both killed instantly. The police are outside in the hallway. Do you feel well enough to speak with them?"

"Yes. Thanks for looking after me."

The police officers who entered this room asked me to describe in my own words what had taken place in the courtroom.

I responded as best as I could but really I was just a minor participant in Curtis Jackson's botched attempt to assassinate me.

The police were impressed that I had disguised myself well enough before I entered the court house. Apparently they had already located several witnesses who had seen Jackson waiting near the court house entrance.

I probably would have been murdered if I hadn't taken the precaution of hiding my white hair.

Although I didn't mention this to the police, I was immensely relieved that Johnathan Baxter had been killed by the very man he had extorted into torching my home.

Sometimes Lady Justice had a wry sense of humor.

Judge Carrino came in after the police finished up with me. She just wanted to make sure that I was okay. I thanked her for her concern.

It was just after one o'clock by the time I walked to my vehicle.

I couldn't get away from Crawford County fast enough.

I drove west on Highway 57 and entered Neosho County fifteen minutes later.

Every mile I put between me and Girard felt like another nail pulled out of the coffin of danger which had enveloped me in Crawford County.

I found a pleasant Highway 160 and drove it all the way to Liberal in the southwest corner of Kansas.

Even though darkness had fallen, I was determined to leave Kansas so I drove another thirty-five minutes and reached Guymon, Oklahoma where I found a motel.

As I studied my maps later in the evening, I decided to get back on Interstate 40 tomorrow and drive as far west as I could.

During the day my mind had been focused on my driving but now in the motel room while sipping beer I began reliving the courtroom ordeal over and over.

Never before had I stared down the barrel of a gun.

My inane utterance after the shooting came to mind.

I repeated it out loud.

"I may be a discarded old lawyer, but I'm not dead yet."

A huge smile broke out on my face.

Ain't that the truth!

THE END

ABOUT THE AUTHOR

Donald W. Desaulniers is a Canadian attorney who resides in the picturesque small city of Belleville, Ontario with his lovely British wife, Jane and their cat.

He is a graduate of University of Waterloo (1968) and University of Western Ontario Law School (1971).

Donald operated his sole practitioner law practice in Belleville from 1973 until he retired in 2009.

After retirement Donald took up writing novels as a hobby.

Always a proponent of quantity over quality, Donald has now published more than 120 novels on Amazon, each of which is available as an E-Book and as a Paperback.

OTHER BOOKS BY THIS AUTHOR

SLIMY LAWYER SERIES

SLIMY LAWYER (#1 in Series)
SLIMY SUES AMERICA (#2 in Series)
SLIMY GETS SHAFTED (#3 in Series)
SLIMY GETS DISBARRED (#4 in Series)
SLIMY TASTES THE GOOD LIFE (#5 in Series)
SLIMY LAWYER CHECKS OUT (#6 in Series)

VANISHING LAWYER SERIES

VANISHING LAWYER (A WORLD WITHOUT ME)
VANISHING LAWYER #2 (UNWANTED WITNESS)
VANISHING LAWYER #3 (FUGITIVE ALIEN)
VANISHING LAWYER #4 (SAVING THE PRESIDENT)
VANISHING LAWYER $5 (SWINDLING SENIORS)
VANISHING LAWYER #6 (SAVING TRUMP AGAIN)

WEIRD LAWYER SERIES

WEIRD LAWYER #1 (NOVICE ATTORNEY)
WEIRD LAWYER #2 (TOUGH TIMES)
WEIRD LAWYER #3 (A PINCH OF JEALOUSY)

SARCASTIC LAWYER SERIES

THE WRONG LAWYER (#1 in Series)
SNARKY LAWYERS (#2 in Series)

LAWYER MURDER MYSTERIES

STUBBORN LAWYER (A CANADIAN MYSTERY)
DISCARDED LAWYER (BUT NOT DEAD YET)
SHUT THAT LAWYER UP
PARADE OF DEAD LAWYERS
LUCKY LAWYER
DIE NOW OLD MAN
THE TWIN SHADOWS
TERRORIST LAWYER

LAWYER NOVELS WITH ROMANTIC THEMES

WIN THE CHILD, WIN THE MOTHER (A COZY ROMANCE)
TOMMY TURDLETTE (NEW LAWYER IN TOWN)
THE LAWYER AND THE PRINCESS (A LOVE STORY)
LOCKDOWN LAWYER
BEVY OF BEAUTIES (FINDING LOVE AFTER LOSS)
NAÏVE LAWYER
LOATHING THE LAWYER, LOVING THE LAWYER

REVENGE DELAYED
THE LIPPY LAWYER'S ROMANCE
THE CHEAPSKATE TWINS
LOVE SEDUCES A FOOL
A RETIRED LAWYER'S DOOMED ROMANCE
BROKE, DISGRACED AND ALONE (A ROMANCE)

OTHER LAWYER NOVELS

CARJACKED LAWYER (A TRAVEL NIGHTMARE)
LAWYER HEAVEN
REVILED LAWYER
FEISTY OLD LAWYERS (BITING BUREAUCRACY)
RICH LAWYER, POOR PRIEST
LADY LUCK LOVES LAWYERS
LAWYER IN THE TOILET
THE CHRISTMAS LAWYER
THE LORD SNATCHES AWAY
FAKE LAWYER
BUYING REDEMPTION
THE LAWYER'S MUSLIM NEIGHBORS
TEMPTING THE GOOD LAWYER

OTHER ROMANCE NOVELS

NO COLLEGE DEGREE, NO PROBLEM (A LOVE STORY)
JOBLESS CHRISTMAS (A TRAVEL ROMANCE)
SWEET ROMANCE BACK HOME
LOVE SAVES A LONER

NOVELS WITH SUPERNATURAL THEMES

FAILED LAWYER, POMPOUS ANGEL
DIVERGENT LAWYER
ALIEN SPECTATORS

HAUNTED FUNERAL HOME SERIES

HAUNTED FUNERAL HOME #1 (GORGEOUS GHOST)

HAUNTED FUNERAL HOME #2 (GHOST DETECTIVES)
HAUNTED FUNERAL HOME #3 (IRRATIONAL GUILT TRIP)

SECOND LIFE SERIES

YOUNG AGAIN (BOOK 1 IN SECOND LIFE SERIES)
YOUNG YET OLD (BOOK 2 IN SECOND LIFE SERIES)
SECOND CHANCE AT LOVE (BOOK 3 IN SECOND LIFE SERIES)

UNDERCOVER HILLBILLY MYSTERY/ACTION SERIES

UNDERCOVER HILLBILLY #1 (A FINANCIAL MYSTERY)
UNDERCOVER HILLBILLY #2 (MURDER SUSPECT)
UNDERCOVER HILLBILLY #3 (A STINKING MYSTERY)
UNDERCOVER HILLBILLY #4 (ANOTHER STRANGE MYSTERY)
UNDERCOVER HILLBILLY #5 (MISSING HALF-BROTHER)
UNDERCOVER HILLBILLY #6 (DANGEROUS ADVERSARY)

TY WARD ADVENTURE SERIES

TY WARD HITS AMERICA (#1 in Series)
TY WARD'S HOLIDAY FROM HELL (#2 in Series)
TY WARD'S NEXT WAR (#3 in Series)
DEADLY WITNESS (#4 in Series)
A YOUNG HOOKER'S THANKS (#5 in Series)
TY WARD'S LAST WAR (#6 in Series)
TY WARD'S SHATTERED PEACE (#7 in Series)
TY WARD'S ROUGH JUSTICE (#8 in Series)
TY WARD'S LOCKDOWN RESCUE (#9 in Series)
TY WARD'S FINAL DEFIANCE (#10 in Series)

WARD JONES ACTION SERIES

WARD JONES #1 (FLEDGLING PREDATOR)
WARD JONES #2 (DAMSELS IN DISTRESS)

OTHER ACTION NOVELS

ELUSIVE WITNESS (HARD TO KILL)
STARTING OVER (DANGER IN MISSOURI)
LADY INJUSTICE (FALSELY ACCUSED)
UNQUALIFIED DETECTIVE (A FINANCIAL MYSTERY)
TRAILER PARK REVENGE (CRIME THRILLER)
CROSSING A RICH MAN (TURNING THE TABLES)
VILE FAMILIES
THE LEFT TACKLE'S CHRISTMAS
ESCAPE FROM EVERYTHING
MARTY MARCOTTES REVOLVING LIFE
FIFTY YEARS LATER (HITCHHIKING IN DONALD TRUMP'S AMERICA)

YOUNG ADULT NOVELS

YOUNG BUT NOT STUPID
CELESTIAL COINCIDENCE
MYSTERY OF THE OLD DESK

NON-FICTION ESSAY

FLUSHING AMERICA DOWN THE TOILET (MISMANAGEMENT, GREED AND "LAWFARE")

NOVELS WRITTEN UNDER PEN NAME "DURWARD GARBAGE"

TOO RICH TOO YOUNG
ANGELA SEVEN (A COGNITIVE ROBOT)
OLD LAWYER, NEW TOWN
TRIPLE GARBAGE (THREE SHORT NOVELS)
WRONG PLACE, WORST TIME
ABANDONED ALIEN (SPACE ALIENS FOR DONALD TRUMP)
GOLDEN CHAOS (STOCK MARKET MELTDOWN)
NASTY MAN (MR. JERK)
ALMOST A LAWYER

SQUANDERING MY FORTUNE
REVENGE FROM HER GRAVE
LAWYER ON THE RUN (PANHANDLING ATTORNEY)
SCORNFUL FAMILY (EATING INSULTS)

NOVELS WRITTEN UNDER PEN NAME "LANCE MAJESTIK"

LOVE LOTTERY LOSER
JUST NOT GOOD ENOUGH
DAMAGED GOODS (A LOVE STORY)
COLD CASE LAWYER
UNVACCINATED OLD LAWYER (REBEL WITHOUT A JAB)
BETTER TIMES (A COMEBACK STORY)
OLD MIND, YOUNG BODY (BODY SWITCH)
LOVE IN OLEAN (AN AMERICAN ROMANCE)
UNDERCOVER TRUCKER (AN AMERICAN MYSTERY)
CRAZY OLD LAWYER (A TALKING SKIN TAG)
LOVE MOCKS A LIMP DICK (WAR OF THE SEXES)

www.ingramcontent.com/pod-product-compliance
Lightning Source LLC
LaVergne TN
LVHW010655110826
845149LV00014B/3098